"Once My Father's On The Mend, I'm Going Back To Sydney," Gabrielle said. "Don't Forget That."

"You've already made that clear." But Damien was more than satisfied.

For the moment.

"I think I'll go to my room. Goodnight."

Damien inclined his head. "Goodnight, Gabrielle," he said, watching her walk away with a sway to her hips that would draw any man's attention. Yet he wasn't just *any* man. He'd been her lover, if not her confidant.

He could feel an odd sort of anger simmering beneath the surface. An anger he wasn't ready to face. Perhaps he'd *never* have to face it…once he had enough of her body.

Dear Reader,

This is my third book in the AUSTRALIAN MILLIONAIRES series, and I can't begin to tell you how wonderful it's been to write for the Silhouette Desire line. I love writing stories where the hero is rich and compelling and the heroine gorgeous and feisty.

And like my first two books, this story is set in Darwin, in the torrid zone north of Australia, where I lived for many years. How fitting it seems, then, to have my heroine, Gabrielle, return home to Darwin after a long absence. Despite hiding a tragic secret, Gabrielle falls in love all over again with Damien, and it proves to be just what she needs. She realizes she has come home in more ways than one.

I trust you will enjoy this story of a prodigal daughter and a powerful executive, who find each other as difficult to resist as this city in the heart of the tropics. I see it as a fitting end to the series and I hope you do, too.

Happy reading!

Maxine

MAXINE SULLIVAN

THE EXECUTIVE'S VENGEFUL SEDUCTION

Silhouette Desire

Published by Silhouette Books

America's Publisher of Contemporary Romance

SILHOUETTE BOOKS

ISBN-13: 978-0-373-76818-9
ISBN-10:   0-373-76818-4

THE EXECUTIVE'S VENGEFUL SEDUCTION

Visit Silhouette Books at www.eHarlequin.com

Printed in U.S.A.

Recent books by Maxine Sullivan

Silhouette Desire

*The Millionaire's Seductive Revenge #1782
*The Tycoon's Blackmailed Mistress #1800
*The Executive's Vengeful Seduction #1818

*Australian Millionaires

MAXINE SULLIVAN

credits her mother for her lifelong love of romance novels, so it was a natural extension to want to write her own romances for her own and others' enjoyment. She's very excited about seeing her work in print and is thrilled to be the second Australian to write for the Silhouette Desire line.

Maxine lives in Melbourne, Australia, but over the years has traveled to New Zealand, the U.K. and the U.S.A. In her own backyard, her husband's job ensured they saw the diversity of the countryside, including spending many years in Darwin in the tropical north. She is married to Geoff, who has proven his hero status many times over the years. They have two handsome sons and an assortment of much-loved, previously abandoned animals.

Maxine would love to hear from you and can be contacted through her Web site at www.maxinesullivan.com.

To Kaz Delaney and Sandra Allan
Firm friends, wonderful writers.
Thanks for the laughs, ladies.

One

Damien Trent acknowledged two things when Gabrielle Kane stepped from the elevator and walked along the corridor toward her office.

She was even more gorgeous than he remembered.

And he'd been a fool to let her go.

"Hello, Gabrielle," he said, straightening away from the wall, his gaze sliding over the soft gray material of her pantsuit that hugged her breasts and clung to her hips, down to the matching strappy sandals. She'd never looked more elegant and feminine than she did right now.

Her blond head shot up from searching through her purse, and her steps faltered. She paled. "My God! Damien?"

"You remembered?" he drawled, then felt something shift inside his chest when those blue eyes met his full-on. For a split second time reversed itself to five years ago. She'd walked into that business function with her father, and their eyes had met across the room, jolting him, making him want her.

Just like they were doing now.

She moistened her mouth, then appeared to pull herself together. "How could I forget?"

"That's something we have in common, then." He moved closer, pleased to see two spots of color rush into her smooth cheeks. "You've grown very beautiful, Gabrielle."

Her delicate chin angled. "Is this a social visit, Damien? You're a long way from home."

He mentally pulled back from wanting her. He was here for a reason. "We need to talk."

"After five years?"

His mouth tightened. She'd been the one to leave *him*. "It's important, Gabrielle."

Alarm flashed in her eyes, then was banked. "It's my father, isn't it?" she said, her tone without inflection now, but he'd seen her immediate reaction. She still cared for the father who'd cut her off after she'd walked out.

He cupped her elbow. "Let's go into your office," he said, feeling the slenderness beneath his palm, conceding that he'd missed touching her.

She turned away and with a shaky hand that was a dead giveaway she unlocked the door to a suite of offices with a sign reading Events by Eileen—The Events Organizer.

He followed her through the main reception area

and into another office, taking in the plush carpet and quality furniture and fittings. "You seem to have done well for yourself."

She walked around the desk and stood with her back to the large glass window, a breathtaking view of the Sydney Harbor Bridge and Opera House behind her. "Let's not pretend you don't already know all about me, Damien. I'm sure whatever report you had done on me must have told you what I do and who I work for." She crossed her arms, her face closed. "Just say what you have to say."

So. She was going to play it cool now, was she? It didn't surprise him. She'd always been a mixture of fire and ice. It was one of the things he'd liked about her— all that passion beneath a cool exterior.

He inclined his head at the high-backed leather chair behind her desk. "You might want to sit."

"I'd rather stand," she said, but her shoulders went back, as if preparing for a blow.

There was no easy way to say this. "Your father's had a stroke, Gabrielle," he said, hearing her gasp, seeing the shock she couldn't hide now. "It caused a cerebral hemorrhage in his brain. It was touch-and-go so they had to operate."

She swallowed hard. "Is he…"

"No, he's not dead. They're hopeful he'll pull through and will recover fully in time."

"Oh God," she murmured, all pretence gone now as she finally sank onto her chair.

He watched her, seeing the whiteness of her skin and the way she bit her bottom lip, and he knew he'd done the right thing by coming to get her. "My private jet's ready when you are."

She blinked up at him. "What?"

"You'll be coming home to Darwin to see your father."

She shook her head. "No...I can't."

His mouth thinned. "He's your father, Gabrielle."

She made a choking sound. "Obviously that hasn't worried him too much these past five years."

It was one thing to ignore your father's existence when he was in good health, but Russell had come close to death. It was time they sorted things out between them. Damien had told Russell the same thing not long before his stroke, when the other man appeared to be fretting over the loss of his daughter. Perhaps Russell sensed something had been about to happen.

"*You* were the one who walked out on him," he pointed out. "Your father found that hard to forgive."

"Perhaps I find it hard to forgive a few things, too," she said, remaining firm.

He was instantly alert. "Such as?"

A wary look suddenly entered her eyes. "It doesn't matter."

"Obviously it does or you wouldn't have mentioned it."

She looked across the desk at him. "Nothing can change the past now. Let's just say that when I left home five years ago I never looked back."

He arched a brow. "*Never?* I find that hard to believe."

She shrugged her slim shoulders and leaned back in her chair. "That's your problem, Damien. Not mine."

Her comment irritated him. "You walked out on me, too," he reminded her silkily.

Her chin rose in the air. "And did *you* find that hard to forgive?"

His jaw clenched. "Your note was sufficient."

"I'm glad you think so," she said with a touch of sarcasm.

He scowled as her comment slammed into him. "You said you wanted to end our affair," he reminded her. "You also said not to try and change your mind."

"And it suited you to believe me, didn't it?"

"Are you saying you lied?" he demanded, his stomach knotting.

Her eyelids flickered, as if she knew she was in dangerous waters. She sighed. "No. It *was* the truth. It was over between us."

He stared hard for a moment as something centered inside his chest. Things were far from over between them. He'd subconsciously realized that when she'd stepped out of the elevator and walked toward him like a vision from heaven.

"No, I don't think it was over at all," he said quietly.

She stiffened. "Really? You obviously didn't think that at the time."

"True. But we had other priorities back then."

She inclined her head but couldn't hide a hint of relief in her eyes. "Yes, we both had a lot of things going on in our lives."

"And I let that get in the way of what was important." He paused. "Things have changed."

She looked startled. "Changed?"

Now that he'd seen her again, he would have to

work her out of his system. In the most pleasurable way, of course.

"It's time to come home, Gabrielle. Your father needs you." Hell, *he* suddenly needed her, too.

Her gaze dropped, and she began to smooth her palms over the front of her silky jacket. Then she looked up as if making a decision. "I'm sorry. Please tell my father I wish him well, but I won't be coming back."

That wasn't acceptable. "And if he dies?"

She winced, then whispered, "Don't."

He couldn't let himself soften toward her. Not right now. He had a job to do. "You have to face facts. Your father is seriously ill. He needs to see you."

"Damien, I can't…I…"

"Not even for your mother's sake?"

Her mouth dropped open, her eyes widened. "Wh-what? My mother? When did you talk to my mother?"

"Caroline came home a couple of days ago when she heard about your father's stroke."

Gabrielle clenched her hands together. "No, she would never forgive him." Her mother would *never* have gone back to her father. When Caroline left, she'd sworn the marriage was over forever.

"She did. And I think you should, too."

"You're lying. This is a trick."

"No tricks, I swear. Gabrielle, your mother asked that I come and get you. She needs you right now."

She flinched. "That's not fair."

"I didn't say it was," he said as he was jabbed by an old heartache. Despite everything that had gone on, at least Gabrielle had parents who cared about her. She wasn't totally nonexistent to them, unlike his own parents. She had a second chance with her family. He doubted his parents would have even *wanted* a second chance. They'd been too involved with themselves...too selfish to consider that their son might just need some of their attention.

Just the thought of it made the muscles at the back of his neck tense. "Look, if you can't come back for your father, then do it for your mother's sake."

She glared at him. "I just can't walk out of here and leave everything to the others. This is a thriving business. We've got some major events coming up."

"I'm sure they can cope without you."

"That's not the point."

"Then what is?" he challenged. She was only making excuses and they both knew it.

She held his gaze for a long moment, then her eyes clouded over and she sighed with surrender. "Okay, I'll come home. But I'm only staying until my father's out of danger."

"Deal." By then he would have her in his bed again and out of his system once and for all.

The thought was completely satisfying.

Long after they were airborne and heading toward Darwin in the Northern Territory of Australia, Gabrielle finished making numerous calls to explain the situation to her clients, then turned off her cell phone to take a break from it all. Before the plane had left Sydney, she'd spoken to Eileen, who'd been supportive of her situation and had made her promise to phone as soon as she was settled.

Dear Eileen. If it hadn't been for the older woman taking her in and treating her like one of her daughters, Gabrielle didn't think she would be as "together" as she was now. Eileen had helped her through so much.

And so had Lara and Kayla, Eileen's daughters. Not only had she been homeless on her arrival in Sydney, but if it wasn't for all three, she would've had to swallow her pride and call her father for help when she'd been in that car accident.

Her heart wrapped in pain, she looked over at Damien Trent, sitting opposite her reading some business papers he'd taken out of his briefcase. If he only knew... Oh God. No, she wouldn't think about that. She'd think about him instead. That would give her something to do.

In his early thirties, he looked as trim and taut as ever, with dark hair and moss-green eyes that always made her catch her breath. He was a lethal combination of manhood.

Her Damien.

The man she'd loved without question five years ago. The man she'd let glimpse her soul. The man she'd have died for. How *had* she found the courage to walk away from him, knowing she was carrying his child?

Yet how could she have stayed when she'd known he hadn't loved her? Their relationship had never been about emotional depth. Not on his part, anyway.

Oh, she'd had no doubt he would have married her once he'd known she was pregnant. But she hadn't wanted that. Not after her father's drunken rage that night telling her to go, when she'd decided then and there that she'd rather her child not have a father at all, than one who hadn't loved its mother. She just hadn't been able to bear the thought of Damien treating her with disdain in front of their child in the years to come. *She'd* been that child with her own parents, and it wasn't a nice feeling.

No, it had been better to cut the ties back then. And from that point on she'd decided she had to stand guard and protect herself from hurt. Love brought too much pain, and she'd wanted nothing more to do with letting anyone so deeply into her heart. And she hadn't.

Until today.

Until Damien had stepped back into her life.

All at once she realized Damien's eyes were upon her. "Everything okay?" he asked, watching her with a light in his eyes that went beyond the sexual, as if he were trying to decipher her thoughts. It made her uncomfortable.

She nodded and turned away, looking out the small window at the blue sky surrounding them, then down at the unimaginable vastness below. They'd left the red dust of the Outback behind some time ago, and now she could see greenery beneath them, growing increasingly greener with each mile, and the closer they got to the coast.

Then time passed and not far in the distance, she could just catch sight of the ocean at the "Top End" of Australia. She sat there for ages absorbing it all, letting it wash over her. This was where she'd been born… where she'd grown up…been happy and sad…passion-ate and heartbroken.

"You're home," Damien said as the plane swept around over the ocean then banked toward the runway.

Beneath them the city of Darwin glistened in the hot tropical sun.

A lump swelled in her throat and she had to blink rapidly. Damien was right, no matter how much she'd denied it to herself all these years. This was home. And home was where her heart was.

It always had been.

Two

Once Damien's plane landed they stepped straight through the invisible sheet of humidity and into a waiting BMW, before speeding through the Darwin suburbs toward the private hospital.

Gabrielle tried to hold her apprehension and worry at bay, but all she could think about now was her father. All these years she'd believed she'd prepared herself for news like this, but now she knew that wasn't possible. The emotional distance she'd worked so hard to maintain was going down the drain. No matter what had gone on between them, he was still her father and she loved him despite everything, and the thought of him dead brought a lump to her throat.

As for her mother, she was still amazed Caroline Kane had returned home to be a wife again. Her mother had been a well-paid doormat to her rich husband, but infidelity was the one thing she hadn't been able to accept. Caroline had been distraught when she'd left the house for good after discovering that Russell had been having an affair with his secretary. She was too upset even to take her teenage daughter with her, even though Gabrielle had begged her.

Repeatedly.

God, did she really have the courage to face them both again? She knew so little about them now. They were her flesh and blood, yet they'd hurt her a great deal. How was she to treat them? Like parents? Like strangers?

Dear God, did any of that matter right now anyway? she wondered as she rode the elevator in silence, her senses conscious of Damien's strong presence, the scent of aftershave a vivid reminder of being in his arms all those years ago.

But once they stepped out of the elevator and into the corridor on her father's floor, she shook off her reaction to Damien's closeness when an attractive woman stepped out of the room ahead of them. As if in slow motion, Gabrielle watched the woman turn toward them. And shock ran through her.

"Mum?" she murmured.

The woman froze. Her eyes widened and her mouth opened, only nothing came out.

Gabrielle stared back. Gone was the pretty but drab woman who'd always worn sedate clothes and her brunette hair in a bun. In her place stood a vibrant fifty-year-old woman with a stylishly cut blond bob and clothes to match.

Suddenly Caroline rushed forward. "Gabrielle!" she cried, and wrapped her arms around her daughter tightly.

Gabrielle couldn't breathe. She stood stiffly. One part of her wanted to sink into the embrace and acknowledge she'd missed this feeling of belonging that went bone deep. This was her mother after all. The woman who'd given birth to her.

It was also the woman who'd left her teenage daughter to cope alone with an increasingly volatile father, she reminded herself.

Caroline pulled back, tears in her eyes. "Oh, my goodness. I can't believe it's you, darling." She blinked rapidly, not seeming to notice Gabrielle's lack of response. "Let me look at you. You're beautiful." Caroline glanced at Damien with a watery look in her eyes. "She's beautiful, isn't she, Damien?"

Gabrielle forced herself to glance at Damien, seeing a hard but admiring look in his eyes before he gave her mother a slight smile.

"Yes, she is, Caroline. Very beautiful."

Despite the moment, his comment sent a tingle through her that she didn't appreciate. She'd always known he'd found her attractive. He'd totally swept her off her feet five years ago, but hearing him say it now after so long away from him made her cheeks grow warm.

"Oh, wait until your father knows you're here," Caroline said excitedly. "It'll be the best medicine."

At the mention of her father, anguish came rushing back. "How is he, Mum? What did the doctors say?"

Caroline squeezed her arm. "Darling, he's doing better than expected."

"Thank God."

"Yes, thank God," Caroline said in a shaky voice. Then she reached up to Damien and gave him a quick kiss on the cheek. "And thank you for bringing my daughter home, Damien. I can't tell you how much this means to me and Russell."

"She was happy to come." He turned toward Gabrielle with mocking eyes. "Weren't you, Gabrielle?"

Gabrielle held his gaze, but her face felt tight. "Yes," she lied.

For the first time her mother seemed to notice Gabrielle's lack of warmth. The light in her eyes dimmed. "Darling, I know we have a lot to say to each other," she said cautiously. "But perhaps that can wait until later? Let's just get through this first."

Gabrielle nodded, thankful for her mother's suggestion. The past didn't disappear just because her father was so ill, but neither was this the right time to air grievances.

Caroline put on a bright face. "Good. Now let's go take a peek at your father," she said, heading back to the room she'd just exited. "He's not supposed to have any visitors except me, but I'm sure it's okay for you to just see him for a moment." At the door she stopped to look at Gabrielle. "Prepare yourself, darling. He's not his best at the moment."

Her mother was right, Gabrielle decided, standing beside her father's hospital bed a little while later. Her eyes misted over as she looked down at his prone body, the white sheets and bandage around his head highlighting his ashen skin, his body thinner than she remembered.

Gently she reached out and touched his cheek. He

moved his head slightly but didn't waken, and she gave a soft cry. It was as if he knew she was there.

Just then the nurse came into the room, and in a compassionate tone advised that there should only be one visitor and perhaps Gabrielle and Damien could come back tomorrow.

Gabrielle nodded, then leaned over and kissed her father's cheek, whispering, "I love you, Dad."

Then she felt Damien's hand on her arm and she looked up at him, surprised by the sympathy in his eyes. She let him lead her from the room, her mother behind them.

Outside, Caroline said regretfully, "Darling, I wish I could come home with you but I need to stay by your father's side for a day or two, just until he's out of danger."

Gabrielle understood. "Mum, it's okay. I can stay at the house by myself."

Her mother's eyes filled with worry. "But that's the problem. They'd just started major renovations when this happened to your father, so I've let them continue while I'm sleeping here at the hospital. But a lot of strange men are working around the place and I don't want you alone there."

Gabrielle accepted that. She wasn't sure she'd even wanted to stay at the house anyway. There were too many bad memories. "Then I'll stay at a hotel."

Her mother clicked her tongue. "Oh, but I don't want you staying in some impersonal hotel room, either."

"Mum, I have to stay somewhere," she half joked, then felt a slither of apprehension when she saw Damien's dark brows jerk together.

He turned to her mother. "Don't worry, Caroline.

Gabrielle can stay at my apartment. I'll even rent her a car so she can get around town."

Gabrielle stiffened. "No, that's not necess—" she began until Damien shot her a dark look silencing her.

Her mother's face had already filled with relief. "That's wonderful, Damien. I'll feel so much better knowing you're close by."

He nodded. "You just concentrate on helping Russell get better."

"But—" Gabrielle began again, not wanting to stay within an inch of this man. They'd been lovers. She was still feeling the pull of his attraction. She couldn't live with him, not even for a day.

"It's no trouble, Gabrielle," Damien said in a tone that brooked no objection.

Caroline gave her daughter a heartfelt hug goodbye. "Darling, let Damien take care of you for a while. Ohh, I'm so glad you're here. And your father will be, too, once he wakes up." Gabrielle wanted to say she didn't need to be taken care of, but Caroline was already kissing Damien on the cheek again. "Look after my baby, Damien. She's precious to me."

"I will."

Just then another nurse went inside the room, and it was obvious her mother was anxious to follow. Gabrielle knew there was nothing for it but to put her own worries aside. "Mum, go back to Dad. I'll see you tomorrow."

"Thanks, darling," Caroline said warmly before she slipped back inside the room.

Then it was just her and Damien again.

Just as it would be at his apartment.

Sharp anxiety twisted inside her, making her testy. "You've got a nerve telling my mother I'll be staying at your place. I'd prefer a hotel."

Displeasure furrowed his brow as he took her arm and started toward the elevator. "You heard Caroline. She's worried about you and wants to know you're safe."

"With *you?*" she scoffed.

"You're always safe with me, Gabrielle." He captured her eyes with his. "It's yourself you're not sure about."

The breath caught in her lungs, but thankfully the elevator doors slid open and she quickly stepped inside, standing away from him, wishing it wasn't empty.

The doors slid shut, enclosing them alone together. "It would be easier if I stayed in a hotel," she insisted stubbornly, knowing she was fighting a losing battle but determined to fight all the same.

He glanced at his Rolex as if he didn't care one way or the other. "My apartment has a spare bedroom. You may as well use it." Yet when he looked up, his eyes had darkened to a jungle green, and just as untamed.

A quiver surged through her veins. "You didn't have a spare bedroom before," she said stupidly, saying the first thing that came to mind, trying not to let him see her reaction.

"That's because I didn't have this apartment before," he drawled.

She flushed. "Fine," she said, giving in to stop from blathering like an idiot again. "But it's only for a few days and that's all."

A satisfied looked crossed his face, making her even more tense. "That's settled then," he said, just as the elevator stopped and the doors opened so other people could get in with them.

She and Damien moved to the back of the compartment, but she was still very aware of him. She tried to resist the compulsion to look sideways but decided one quick look wouldn't hurt.

And that was her mistake.

His gaze lingered on her figure, making her nipples tighten beneath the light material of her pantsuit. She'd chosen the outfit because it flattered her moderate bustline and slight swell of her hips, and because she always felt good in it. The last thing she'd expected when she'd dressed this morning was an X-ray treatment from a man who'd been her lover and knew every inch of her body.

Oh God. Her staying at his apartment may have been settled, but she had the uneasy feeling nothing else had been settled at all.

Having Gabrielle in his apartment was more than Damien expected on her first day back in town, but he would take it one step at a time. He wanted her in his bed but he also wanted a willing partner and was prepared to wait until she was ready.

It won't be a long wait.

She could fight herself all she wanted, but it was obvious she was fighting a losing battle. She wanted him as much as he wanted her. He could *smell* that want in her…that need of desire. He felt the same. Her scent filled his nostrils…filled his apartment even now.

And all she had done was walk through to the spare

bedroom, he thought with a wry smile as he remembered her cool comment that she'd see him at dinner. But she hadn't been cool inside. He knew the two of them struck sparks off each other and that it was only a matter of time before they burst into flames.

In the meantime he didn't mind playing with matches, he mused as he showered and changed for dinner, then arranged for dinner to be delivered.

Then he sat on the sofa to do some paperwork, though his mind kept flicking to Gabrielle and her parents. He had to admit that Russell hadn't been the best father in the world after Caroline had left a few years earlier. And what had gone on before that, he didn't know. He hadn't known them then, having moved to Melbourne for a few years, building his fortune, only flying back to Darwin every so often to play poker with his best friends, Brant and Flynn.

Then one day he'd decided he missed the tropics and he'd come home for good. Fortuitously, Russell had been looking for a business partner at the time, and *he'd* been looking to make more money. He'd gone on to forge his own company and make his millions. It had worked out well.

Until now.

Until Gabrielle Kane had walked back into his life.

Just like she was doing this very minute as she made an appearance at the living room doorway. She was worth the wait, dressed in a sleeveless, teal-colored crocheted top and long white pants that clung to her gorgeous figure, making her look casual yet stylish.

"Hungry?" he said, putting the papers aside on the sofa and getting to his feet.

"A little."

He started across the open-plan apartment toward the dining table nestled over in the corner. "Everything's ready."

She slowly followed him, then frowned when she saw the table laden with food. "Are others coming?"

"No. Just us. I ordered from the restaurant across the street." The chef *had* gone a little overboard with the array of tropical salads, dishes teeming with prawns and lobster, Tasmanian salmon and barramundi fish. "I told them plenty of seafood," he said, deliberately reminding her that he remembered how partial she'd been to this type of food.

Her eyes brightened, then she flushed. "Thank you, but I doubt I'll do it all justice."

"No problem. My housekeeper will be delighted to take the leftovers off my hands." He held out the chair for her. "Sit here."

She moved forward and did as he suggested. Once she was comfortable, he took his own seat and poured wine into their glasses.

Her gaze darted around the room. "This is a really nice apartment."

"I know. Lucky for me one of my friends married a very talented lady who loves to decorate."

The place hadn't been half-bad before, but Danielle had suggested some ideas and he hadn't had the heart to dissuade her. He and Flynn had smiled at each other as she'd enthusiastically promised a stylishly furnished apartment with class and sophistication that was ideal for executive living. And she'd lived up to that promise.

The open plan of the living and dining area, abundant with natural light, soaked up the magnificent panoramic views of the harbor…her words, not his. She'd done a great job of it.

"It's lovely," Gabrielle agreed.

"Just like you are, Gabrielle," he said, holding her eyes with his. One day soon he would hold her in his arms. And he would show her how lovely he thought she was.

A pulse beat at the base of her throat. "You know, I'm suddenly really hungry," she said huskily, and began piling the food on her plate.

He was too, but it wasn't for food. Dammit, waiting was already harder than he'd expected.

It would be easier once he said what he needed to say. She wasn't going to be so placid then, he decided, as they ate in silence for a while, listening to the soft background music, but eventually he knew he couldn't put this off. She wasn't going to like it.

He raised his glass in a toast. "To you, Gabrielle."

Her eyes widened. "Me?"

"For having the courage to come home again."

She looked pleasantly surprised as she picked up her glass and clinked it against his. "Thank you," she said, a slight catch to her voice that unfurled something soft inside his chest.

He took a sip of wine, then said, "Your mother was pleased to see you today."

"Yes."

"I imagine Russell will be, too."

"Yes."

"Aren't you glad now that you came?"

Her forehead creased a little, her eyes growing puzzled. "Yes, I am."

He rested back against his chair. "And you're happy to be here in Darwin?"

She eyed him with sudden suspicion. "Okay, what's this about, Damien?"

Leaning forward, he placed his wine glass on the table, then dropped the bombshell. "Your cousin has taken control of the Kane Property and Finance Group."

Her cousin was an idiot.

A dangerous idiot.

She gaped at him. "Keiran? How on earth did he get involved in all this?"

Damien's mouth tightened. "Some years ago your father sold forty percent of the company shares to him, that's why."

She sat up straighter. "What! Why would he do that?"

"Russell wanted to keep it in the family if anything happened to him, and Keiran worked on him until he sold him the shares." Damien had advised Russell against it, but the older man seemed to have a blind spot where his nephew was concerned, and now his company that specialized in providing investment property finance here in Australia and the growing Asian market, was paying the price. "Your father also left written instructions with his attorney that if he became incapacitated, then *you* were to get forty percent of the shares as well."

"What!"

"You each now hold forty percent of the Kane Property and Finance Group."

She shook her head. "I don't believe I'm hearing this."

"Believe it."

"Oh my Lord." She sat there for a moment looking stunned.

"Keiran's been at Kane's for some years now and he knows the business. As soon as Russell had the stroke he stepped in and took over. Your cousin was always quick when there was something in it for him."

"I know."

He paused, then, "And that's exactly why you needed to be here."

"Me?"

"Yes."

Her eyes widened. "Good heavens, you don't expect me to step in and start running a multinational company, do you?"

"Why not? Keiran did. He's already made some decisions that would give your father another stroke if he knew, and we can't do a damn thing to stop him." The only person who could stop him was sitting right here. "If you assume control, Keiran will hopefully slink back into his own little office where he can do no more damage."

She stared at him in disbelief. "But Keiran owns as many shares as I do now. He's not going to give up the top job."

Damien could feel his jaw clench. "Let's try him first."

She shook her head, obviously trying to get it clear in her mind. "Hang on. Why didn't you tell me all this back in Sydney?"

"Would you have come home?"

"I don't know," she said, her forehead marred with a

crease. "And I don't understand why my father left *me* forty percent."

"Perhaps he expected you would come back if he needed you. And he *does* need you now, Gabrielle."

A cynical light came into her eyes. "You mean he thought it was a good way of blackmailing me into coming home if he ever needed me." She shook her head. "It's still all about *him*, isn't it?"

Damien ignored that. "Your father wouldn't expect you to take over if you weren't capable."

Her eyebrows shot up as realization dawned on her. "Oh, so he's been keeping tabs on me, too."

He had no idea, but it was highly likely. "Russell doesn't always take me into his confidence." The older man had been a friend and mentor but he'd never spoken about his daughter until recently. "Look, I'll help you. I've delegated some of my own business dealings to others. I've got the time."

A flicker of apprehension crossed her face. "To work with me every day, you mean?"

"Yes." And if he got to make love to her sooner, all the better.

Her beautiful blue eyes hardened and narrowed. "What's in it for you, Damien?"

He returned her look with a level one of his own. "I want to help Russell. I owe him a lot."

Seconds ticked by. "That's commendable of you," she said somewhat sourly.

His mouth tightened. "I admire Russell and what he's achieved."

"And look at the price he paid for it," she pointed out.

"He lost his wife and then his daughter, and now he's losing his company. Don't admire him, Damien. Pity him."

"So why aren't *you?*" he challenged, and saw her startled look. "Come on, Gabrielle. Tell me. Why aren't *you* showing your father some pity?"

She bridled. "I'm here, aren't I?"

"Under protest."

She dropped her gaze to the table. "That may be so, but I do love my father nonetheless." Her eyelashes lifted. "But even if I wanted to help more, there are limits to what I can do."

"How do you know? You haven't even tried."

Her lip curled with sarcasm. "Your understanding amazes me."

He took his time before saying what needed to be said. "You're the only one who can save the company from ruin, Gabrielle."

"What about my mother?" she said as sudden hope swept across her face. "Perhaps I can sign over the shares to her and she could stop Keiran from taking over the company. She only needs to put in an appearance and you could do the rest."

"You would ask that of your mother? When she's having a hard enough time as it is?"

"Yet it's okay to ask it of me?" She grimaced, and a slight flush tinged her cheeks. "That sounded selfish. I didn't mean it like that."

He inclined his head. "Caroline's got enough on her plate looking after your father right now."

She raised her chin. "And if I don't choose to be a part of this?"

"I don't think you'd forgive yourself if your parents lost everything."

She exhaled a long, ragged breath. "You really know how to tighten the thumb screws, don't you?"

"Sometimes we have to do things we don't want to do but we do them anyway."

"Okay, okay, I'll try," she snapped. "But once my father's on the mend, I'll be leaving and going back to Sydney. Don't forget that."

"You've already made that clear." But he was more than satisfied.

For the moment.

She placed her napkin on the table and pushed to her feet. "Somehow I've lost my appetite. I think I'll go to my room. Good night."

It was more than clear she wanted time alone. Time he could afford to give her.

He inclined his head. "Good night, Gabrielle," he said, watching her walk away with a sway to her hips that would draw any man's attention. Yet he wasn't just *any* man. He'd been her lover, if not her confidant.

And she'd walked out on him without a proper good-bye. It had left a loss he only recognized now that he'd seen her again. A loss that went deeper than he'd expected. And because of it, he could feel an odd sort of anger simmering beneath the surface. An anger he wasn't ready to face. Perhaps once he had enough of her body he'd *never* have to face it.

Three

Gabrielle retired to the spare bedroom and stood looking out the window at the harbor. Being around Damien wasn't conducive to being clear-minded. He always seemed to be watching her, waiting for her to lower her guard. And keeping up that guard was exhausting when she had other things to think about.

God, it was mind-boggling that her father had given her forty percent of the shares in the business. Of course, she thought cynically, he hadn't been able to bring himself to give her the remaining sixty percent of the shares—not that she wanted them.

No, he'd been hedging his bets. He'd given her limited control of the business, but had withheld twenty percent of the shares for himself just in case his incapacitation had proven temporary. And that was predictably her father. He could never let go of total control.

As for Keiran holding forty percent of the shares, well, that was a justified worry. Her cousin had always had his eye on the main chance, no matter what had been at stake, whether it be tripping her up as a kid so he could jump in the swimming pool first, or trying to suck up to her father during her parents' separation. She had no doubt Keiran was capable of anything. She disliked him intensely. He was the one person who should *not* be in charge of a multimillion-dollar business.

As for Damien, it was typical he hadn't told her about this before now. If she didn't know him better, she'd think he was just like Keiran, keeping secrets to himself and using them for his own benefit.

Only, she knew he *wasn't* like Keiran.

Not at all.

Damien wasn't underhanded, just arrogant. She couldn't see Damien tripping anyone to get in the pool first. He just wasn't that kind of person. Damien would manipulate to get what he wanted—oh, yes, and he was good at that—but there was a difference. Damien wasn't the type to lie or cheat if confronted over an issue. If Damien said something, he meant it. If he gave his word, he would stand by it.

Heavens, never in her wildest dreams had she imagined she'd ever be spending another night sleeping under Damien's roof. And in separate bedrooms, too. And that was just as well. He'd been a sensual man when she'd met him and she knew he hadn't changed. She could still feel the sensuality rolling off him in waves. Even now she remembered the force of his desire from the day she'd walked into that function with her father and she'd felt the pull of a man's eyes from across the room.

Damien.

It had been that strong.

But that's all it had ever been with him. She'd only ever known him in the physical sense, never the emotional one. For two glorious months over a tropical summer it had been all about sex and attraction on his part, while she'd fallen headlong in love with him.

And she'd wanted him to love her in return, only it was never going to happen. She'd realized that the day she'd left home for good. It had given her the strength not to look back. If she had, she would have weakened and gone running into his arms.

But not into his heart.

It had taken her years to get over him, but time and distance had put things into perspective. It had been lust, not love. Attraction, not affinity. It was important to remember that, she decided as the adrenaline pumped through her veins, taking her a long time to fall asleep. Once she did, exhaustion gave her some blessed relief from the relentless thoughts going through her head, and when she stepped into the kitchen the next morning, she felt more rested than she'd dared hope.

Until she saw Damien standing at the counter, contemplating the mug of coffee in his hands as if it held the secrets to life itself. He obviously hadn't heard her enter because he didn't move. Strange, but he looked sort of…lonely.

She must have made a sound because his head shot up,

and a seductive glint slid straight into his eyes. "Ah, the prodigal daughter has awoken," he drawled, his gaze going over her red sleeveless dress cinched at the waist with a belt of the same material, and matching leather pumps.

"And good morning to you, too," she said coolly, forcing herself to ignore the pull of his physical appearance. So what if he was dressed in dark trousers and a white shirt that looked like they'd been born on him?

A lazy moment passed by as Damien considered her, then he placed his mug on the counter behind him. "I phoned the hospital earlier. Russell's doing as well as expected."

Her heart fluttered with anxiety at the reminder of her father. "Thank you. I was going to call shortly myself." She moved toward the percolator on the counter, badly needing her morning cup of coffee. "I plan on going to see him soon."

"They said not to come until this afternoon. Apparently they've got a couple of doctors checking him over this morning." He must have seen her give a start. "Your mother said it was nothing to worry about."

Her panic subsided as she poured coffee into a cup. "Then I can go see Keiran instead. I planned on it, anyway."

"Aah, so that's why you're dressed like that."

Something in his voice made her look up, and she found his eyes sliding over her again, making her catch her breath. She put the coffeepot back with a shaky hand and tried to act casual. "I'm not about to go into my father's office in jeans and a tank top."

"Might get some favorable comments."

"More likely they'd direct me to the janitor's room," she quipped, looking at him over the top of her coffee cup.

All at once he smiled. A rare smile that knocked her off balance. For a moment she could only stare at him across the width of the room.

Then that smile faded and something in those eyes darkened and he moved forward, making her heart drop to her knees. He stopped right in front of her, took the cup out of her hand then placed it on the counter beside her.

"It's been a long time, Gabrielle," he said huskily, in a voice so Australian, so thick and delicious, it swirled around her heart like a long-lost friend. "Miss me?"

She swallowed. "Does a bear miss a toothache?" she managed to say, the breathlessness in her voice disturbing her.

He gave a soft laugh and slid his hands over her shoulders with an ease that only an ex-lover can have. "Hmm. I like your hair this length." Provocatively, one finger coiled around some blond strands that curled below her neck. "It suits you."

She shivered as his warm breath wafted over her and wrapped her in its minty scent. It seemed like only yesterday when she would have leaned into the hard wall of his chest and relished his strength. And only yesterday that they had made love with a passion that had stolen her breath away.

"You're even more beautiful than I remember," he murmured, his hands sliding down to her hips.

Up close, his green gaze was a caress, his male scent too enticing, the tension between them building, overwhelming her, restricting her breathing, making her forget that never again had she wanted to be close enough to see into the irises of his emerald eyes…or the grain of his skin as it weaved and dipped its way over a strong nose and lean cheekbones…nor had she ever wanted to touch the fullness of his lips, to know she'd once ached to have them on her body.

"Stop it," she whispered, hating herself for letting him affect her like this.

"Stop what?"

"Damien…"

"Gabi…"

Gabi. He'd only ever called her that once before. He'd been thrusting inside her and she'd been welcoming each plunge of his body. They'd reached their climax together. It had been the only time she'd felt his equal, and not some young woman who'd been the daughter of his business partner.

All at once she had to get out of the kitchen.

It was too small.

There wasn't enough air.

She pushed his hands off her and spun away, heading for the door, not even sure if Damien had hired a car yet for her, but willing to catch a cab if necessary. "I need to see Keiran…at the office…in case he goes out." She was babbling but couldn't seem to stop herself.

He came up behind her, putting his hand on her arm, stopping her but not in a forceful way. "I'm coming with you," he rasped, the huskiness still in his voice, the desire still glittering from the depths of those green eyes.

His touch sent a tingle along her spine. "There's no need."

His mouth tightened and he dropped his hand. "I said I'd help and I will. Don't underestimate Keiran. There's power in numbers, Gabrielle."

She sent him a wary glance. "I know my own cousin."

"Then you know you need me with you."

As much as she didn't want it to be, what he said was true. She abruptly nodded her head. "Okay, but I need to get that rental car later for my own use," she said, giving in but perhaps not as gracefully as she could, and that was more to do with needing to get away from Damien's presence than *not* needing him to help her deal with Keiran.

But in the confines of his car, her mind couldn't stop from going back to Damien. She realized that being a woman desired by him was more dangerous to her now than five years ago. Now he would want more than girlish enthusiasm in his bed. He'd want a woman's response, slow and deliberate, not a rushed and naive eagerness. And he'd expect her to be a mature partner, able to handle a sexual relationship without too much emotion. It was a world of difference to five years ago.

She pushed all her thoughts to the side as they walked into the building that housed the head office of her father's company. The first person she saw was one of her father's managers she remembered from years ago. He greeted her warmly then expressed sympathy over her father's condition.

"Thank you, James. I'm glad to see you're still here."

The older man's eyes flicked to Damien then back to her. "Not for long I'm afraid. I've accepted a position with another company. I finish up at the end of the week."

Dismay filled her. "Oh, I'm sorry to hear that."

"Gabrielle, I've got nothing to lose by saying this. I've always enjoyed working for your father, but it's going to be a while before he's back on his feet. I'm sorry but I can't work with *him* until that happens."

"You mean Keiran?" she said to clarify, but knowing all Damien had told her was true.

James nodded. "I don't mind saying I think that man's going to ruin the company with his ideas. And I'm not the only one leaving, either. There are two heads of departments who have put their resignation in and another planning on it." He clicked his tongue. "They're men who are going to be taking a whole lot of experience and knowledge with them when they go, I'm afraid."

She tried to look confident. "James, that's why I'm here. My father wanted me to take over if anything happened to him and that's what I'm going to do."

Relief flared then died in his eyes. "Keiran isn't going to step aside so easily," he warned.

She squeezed the older man's hand. "Keiran won't have a choice."

But when Damien opened the door to her father's office and Gabrielle saw her cousin sitting behind her father's desk like he owned the place, every instinct inside wanted to tell him to get the hell out of there.

Keiran glanced up at the interruption and for a moment looked like an animal caught in the headlights. Then he went rigid. "Well, well. If it isn't my long-lost cousin." He pasted on a false smile as he stood and came around the desk. "Gabrielle, how nice to see you again."

Her mouth tightened as he pecked at both her cheeks like a chicken. "Keiran, you haven't changed a bit." He was two years older than her, and he'd wielded his older stance often during their childhood.

"You're still the sweetest thing," he joked as he glanced at Damien. But his eyes were wary beneath his blond head and they held a heartless gleam that had been in them since the day he'd been born. Now, here was one person her father *should* have cut off, she thought, suppressing a moment of pain that it had been his own daughter her father had ignored instead.

She stepped away. "What are you doing in here, Keiran?"

His smile flattened. "What do you think I'm doing in here? Someone had to step in when your father had his stroke."

"Then thank you. I appreciate it but I'm here now."

His piercing eyes contrasted sharply with his relaxed stance. "Not so fast. You can't just walk in here and take over."

She arched a brow. "Why not?"

He strode back around the desk. "You've been gone five years. And before that you never worked here in any capacity anyway."

She refused to let him see his comment had hit its mark. "I spent a couple of school holidays working here, remember?"

"And that gives you the experience to run a multinational company dealing in property and finance, does it?"

"From what I hear, I could do better than what you've been doing," she said coolly.

As if a storm was brewing, the air seemed to sizzle with electricity. "I don't know what you mean."

"I mean that from all accounts you're running the company into the ground. All our managers are leaving."

He waved a dismissive hand. "They were old and stale. We need new blood."

She gave a soft gasp. "That's a callous statement."

His lips twisted. "Perhaps I'm a chip off the old block."

She held herself stiffly. "My father would never have dumped his employees."

"Sure? I think if Russell kept them on, it was for his own selfish reasons."

She didn't want him to see that he was probably right, so she ignored that. "Look, I'm here now and I have Damien to help me."

"No."

She blinked. "What do you mean no?"

Keiran's glare resented their presence. "I have every right to be in this office, Gabrielle. Just ask your friend, here. That's why he went to get you to bring you back. Don't fool yourself it was only about your father's stroke."

"I ought to hit you for saying that, Keiran," Damien said, his eyes as cold as dry ice.

"But you can't deny it."

"You're not worth refuting."

Keiran sat on the chair with a smirk. "May I suggest you go and rethink your position. I own forty percent of this company and I intend to take it places Russell never even dreamed about."

Gabrielle gasped, and Damien growled, "You've bitten off more than you can chew, Keiran."

Keiran shrugged. "I'm in charge, Trent, whether you like it or not." He picked up a pen. "Now. If you'll both excuse me I have work to do. Major changes are on my agenda."

Gabrielle stood there for a moment, stunned and shaken. "Don't make too many changes, Keiran. I'll only have to change them back."

He waved a hand at the door. "Don't let me keep you."

For a moment Gabrielle thought Damien might leap across the desk and throw the other man out, but with a pulse ticking in his jaw, he thrust open the door and let her precede him through it.

They didn't speak as they rode the elevator down with another couple to the parking lot beneath the building. But once they were in the BMW she sat while he came around to the driver's side, her mind ticking over. What the devil were they going to do? If indeed they could do anything at all to wrestle the company from Keiran's grip before he did too much damage.

Damien slid onto the driver's seat. "Are you okay?"

She blinked. "Yes, I'm fine," she said, but just as quickly realized she wasn't. Whether it was because Keiran had put such a bad taste in her mouth, she suddenly felt the need to go home to where she'd grown up. All at once she wanted to touch base with something familiar.

"No, I'm not. Damien, take me home please. To my parents' place." She took a shuddering breath. "Just for a little while."

He stared at her, watching her with some indefinable emotion in his eyes, then nodded. "I've got papers in my briefcase. I can work from there."

Sudden resentment grew. Couldn't he see she needed to be alone for a while? "Or you could just leave me there and I'll get a rental car sent around."

His mouth thinned. "I'm not leaving you alone with a group of strangers working around the place."

She glowered at him. "Why not? Frightened I might run off with one of them?"

He swore. "Don't be ridiculous, Gabrielle. You're upset over Keiran. Don't take it out on me."

She sighed. "I'm sorry, you're right. Just take me home, Damien."

He started the car and ten minutes later drove through the open gates of her parents' home that she hadn't seen in five long years. She gazed up at the two-level mansion of grand proportions dozing in the tropical Australian sunshine. She'd grown up playing dolls on that wide balcony around the house. And later she'd sought refuge looking through the large windows of her bedroom over treetop views to the Timor Sea and distant horizon. It had been a wonderful place to grow up. If only her parents hadn't fought all the time in those latter years. If only she'd had a brother or sister to share things with.

Thankfully Damien strode off toward the sound of hammering in the kitchen as soon as they stepped inside, saying he would tell the workmen to take a long break, and Gabrielle left him to it.

It was an odd feeling walking up the sweeping staircase to the second floor. Five years had passed, yet it only seemed like yesterday. But as she pushed the door open to her old bedroom, her mind reeled in confusion.

The room was like a time warp. Everything was the same. The bed she'd often cried her heart out on, despairing over her parents' troubled marriage, was still covered in the same quilt. Posters of some obscure pop star whose name she couldn't even recall still hung on the wall. And even the clothes she'd left behind were still hanging in the wardrobe…almost as if they were waiting for her return.

She swallowed a sob. A new and unexpected warmth surged through her that was a welcome relief after her tussle with her cousin today. If ever she needed proof of her parents' love for her, here it was. They had kept her memory alive.

Just like she did with her own child.

Damien's baby.

A baby she'd miscarried at six months because of the car accident. God, how she wanted to tell Damien about their unborn baby that she'd loved and lost. Only, she knew she couldn't tell him…could never tell him. He may not have cared for her, but she had no doubt he would have cared for their child. And she would never want any person knowing that brand of heartache.

Certainly not the baby's father.

Damien glanced up from his paperwork and saw Gabrielle stroll out onto the patio, then stand looking out beyond the swimming pool, over the manicured lawn and lushly landscaped gardens.

Adrenaline kicked in as he watched the sun beat down on her face, giving a glow to her smooth skin. The high humidity of the November build-up toward the wet season wisped strands of the blond shoulder-length hair at the base of her neck. God, he couldn't get over how beautiful she was. In the past five years he'd made love to other women, some more beautiful than Gabrielle, but none of them had...what was the word he was looking for?

Connected.

Yes, that was it. None of them had connected with something deep inside him the way Gabrielle did. Something fundamental. Something that was grabbing at him even now.

He thrust his papers aside and pushed off the sofa to go to her. "I'm impressed," he said as he stepped through the open patio doors to join her.

She spun around, her face quickly assuming a blank mask that made him want to strip aside all the layers and get to what was truly inside this woman. "You are? With what?"

He went to stand beside her at the balustrade. "You." He saw her start of surprise. "I like the way you stood up to Keiran."

Her mouth curved into an unexpected smile, fascinating him. "Well, now you know. You're not the only one I can stand up to."

He went still, caught by an invisible pull of attraction. "I can see that," he murmured, his gaze dropping to those kissable lips.

Awareness flared in her eyes, and she quickly turned and looked down at the garden instead. "Let's hope my father gets better soon."

"It's going to take some time for your father to recover enough to get back to work." If indeed he came back at all. "Many months at best."

She sighed. "Then there's nothing further I can do here. I may as well leave Keiran to it."

Damien's gut clenched. It wasn't just the thought of Keiran ruining everything for Russell that made his spirits sink. It was the thought of Gabrielle leaving. She would be on her way back to Sydney just as soon as Russell pulled out of danger. A week was probably all she'd stay, and that wasn't good enough. He wanted her in his arms and in his bed. He would settle for nothing less.

Just then an idea clicked inside him and his pulse began to race. It was the answer to the company's prayers. Surprisingly, he wasn't averse to the idea either. Lately, he had been watching Brant and Flynn with their wives and he'd felt like he was missing out on something special that came from being a couple. And Gabrielle was the only woman he could imagine being a couple with.

"Of course, we could always combine our shares and get Keiran out that way," he said quietly.

Her eyes were confused as she turned to face him fully. "I don't understand. How would we do that?"

He captured her eyes with his. "I'm a silent shareholder. I own the other twenty percent."

Her head snapped back. "What!"

"And I have the perfect solution."

She blinked and a wary look crossed her face. "You do?"

"Marry me, Gabrielle," he said smoothly. "Marry me and let's make sure Keiran never takes control of Kane's again."

Four

Gabrielle stared at Damien, unable to believe she was hearing right. "Marriage! To *you?*"

The line of his mouth tightened. "That's the idea."

Her heart constricted. Did he know what he was asking? "But why? I mean, I know you feel my father gave you a helping hand years ago but this is going too far, Damien."

"No. I'd say it's going just far enough." A look of implacable determination crossed his face. "It's the only way to stop Keiran."

She winced inwardly, trying to remember this was about Keiran, not about her and Damien. Yet she and Damien would pay the price. *Again.* Hadn't they already paid enough?

She tilted her head. "But even if we marry, my shares

belong to me and your shares belong to you. It doesn't give us controlling interest."

For a long moment he stared at her. Then, "It does if I sign over eleven percent of my shares to you as a wedding present."

"What!" she exclaimed, giving him a glance of utter disbelief.

He arched a brow. "Can you think of a better way to get Keiran out?"

She swallowed hard. "There must be another way," she said, trying not to let the desperation show in her voice.

"If there is I'd be glad to hear it."

She gathered her wits about her. "Let me talk to Keiran again. I'm sure I can make him see reason."

"Keiran will only see reason if there's something in it for him. And I don't think anything you offer will tempt him away from the top seat, do you?"

He was right. It would take much more than anything she had for Keiran to step aside.

"Of course," Damien drawled, wry amusement entering his eyes. "We could always kill him to get him out of the way."

She glared at him. "This is too serious to joke about."

"Who's joking?" he mocked, but there was a hardness to his tone that bode ill for the other man. "I'm just trying to make you see that marriage between us is the only alternative. It may not be what you want to hear but it's the best there is."

No, she couldn't believe that.

She wouldn't.

"Surely you don't want to get married, Damien? More to the point, surely you don't want to marry *me?*"

"I'm glad you know what I don't want," he snapped. "Actually, it's time I settled down. I'm getting older and I want a wife and…" a moment crept by "…you're the wife I want."

She swallowed hard. For a minute there she'd thought he was going to say he wanted a family with her. She wasn't sure if she were up to that.

But being Damien's wife…

"Would this be a temporary arrangement?" she asked, not considering it but asking all the same.

"No."

Her eyes widened. "You mean…"

"Once we marry, we stay married." A muscle ticked in his cheek. "It's forever, Gabrielle. Remember that."

"I don't think I could forget it," she muttered. Then a hopeful idea came to mind. "Of course, you could always just sign over the eleven percent to me anyway. That would be a good way to repay my father."

"No, the best way to repay your father is for us to marry. A united front will put confidence back in the company for our clients." He paused. "Oh, and Gabrielle. I will want your parents to think this is a real marriage between us."

Her heart thudded inside her chest. "You mean you want them to think we're in *love?*"

He nodded. "Yes. I'll tell your father about me giving you the shares, of course, but only after he's on the mend. I don't want him getting even a hint that we married to stop Keiran from ruining the company. It could set back his recovery."

Damien was right about her father not needing to hear bad news. "But surely my mother should be told the truth?" she questioned, even as she told herself the point was moot.

He shook his head. "No, if we're going to do it, we may as well do it properly. I don't want any slip-ups in front of your father, and with your mother being under a lot of stress, it wouldn't be fair to burden her."

He made it all sound so rational. Yet how could she pretend to be in love with this man? And why the heck was she considering this, anyway?

She lifted her chin. "I'm sorry but I won't marry you, Damien. My father wouldn't want me to go that far."

He arched a brow. "Really? I'm sure Russell would want you to do everything in your power to save all he's built over the years. And that includes marriage to me."

She straightened her shoulders. "Look, you can be a martyr about it, but I will *not* sacrifice myself like this for the sake of the company. Not for my father. And not for my mother, either," she added, preempting him.

His eyes narrowed. "Then what about for all those people who work for your father?"

Her hands clenched. "It's no use, Damien. Just give it up."

"No, you need to give *in*. There are people depending on your decision. People like James. People who have worked for your father for years, not just here in Darwin but all around Australasia. If Keiran destroys the company then there's going to be a hell of a lot of people out of work."

"I can't take responsibility for the whole damn world," she choked. If this was what it was like at the top, then they could have it.

His dark brows jerked together. "Don't swear, Gabrielle."

Her eyes widened. "How can you take this so calmly? This is our *lives* you're talking about ruining."

His face closed up more than usual. "I don't think marriage between us will ruin our lives. We may even enjoy it."

She gave a strangled laugh. "It may not ruin yours, but it will definitely ruin mine. I don't know what you've got planned for the rest of your life, but being married to you isn't on my list."

His green eyes darkened to near black as a hardness rippled through him like a chain reaction. His mouth opened. He went to speak.

And his cell phone rang.

He held her gaze a moment more, watching her. Then he took the phone out of his pocket and answered it. She was just beginning to take a breath when she noticed his gaze shoot to her. She tensed immediately, sensing it must be the hospital.

"We'll be there soon," he said into the phone, then hung up and returned it to his pocket.

"It's my father, isn't it?" she whispered, expecting a blow.

"He's fine. But they've finished some tests and now

he's awake. Your mother said it's a good time to come visit for a couple of minutes."

Intense relief washed over her. "We'd better hurry, then," she said, wishing she'd thought to give her cell phone number to her mother so that she'd always be available if anything happened. Not that she wanted to think about the worst happening, she decided, spinning on her heels to go back through the patio doors, glad to put an end to this discussion with Damien.

"We'll finish this later," he warned.

She had to stand her ground with him. "There's nothing to discuss."

Their eyes met and shock ran through her. There was a firm look on his face that said he wasn't giving up. The thought tore at her insides and made her heart plummet to the depths of her soul. Damien always got what he wanted. It was just a pity he wanted a marriage of convenience with *her*. Dear God, the last thing she wanted was to be a *convenience* to this man.

That thought kept her resolute on the way to the hospital. She had to make sure she kept up her guard against Damien. Always, just when she thought she could hold her own with him, he'd change tack and sweep the rug out from under her. He was a ruthless businessman.

A ruthless *man*.

Just like her father, she reminded herself.

Of course, her father didn't look too ruthless when she stood beside his hospital bed, his hand engulfing hers and a tear slipping down his cheek. Her eyes misted over and she leaned forward to kiss him, but ended up burying her face against his neck, careful not to cause him pain. For a split second all her hurt melted like candle wax. This was her father. And she was his little girl again.

"Gabrielle," his shaky voice rumbled in her ears, and she swallowed hard. It had been so long since she'd heard him say her name so lovingly. Too long.

"Oh, Russell, our baby girl's all grown-up now," Gabrielle heard her mother say. It startled her to hear her parents actually talking civilly to each other for a change.

"Yes," he said gruffly, and squeezed her hand again as if he never wanted to let her go.

Gabrielle took a deep breath and straightened, blinking back tears. Then her gaze fell on Damien and all at once her heart flipped over at the touch of tenderness in the back of those green eyes.

For her.

But Damien tender? Common sense told her that if he did feel any softening toward her, it was because he wanted something from her. She flinched inwardly. Oh, he wanted something all right.

Marriage.

"Sorry," her father mumbled, pulling her thoughts away from her problems with Damien.

"Dad, shh. We'll talk when you're better." Though what she'd say to him, she wasn't sure. Deep down there was still hurt and anger over all that had happened. She couldn't dismiss those feelings easily.

"Sleepy," her father murmured, shutting his eyes.

She kissed his cheek. "Go to sleep then, Dad. I'll be back tomorrow," she said softly, sure he was asleep before she'd even finished speaking.

Her mother's eyes filled with gratitude. "He'll recover well just knowing you're here."

"I'm glad," Gabrielle said, unable to prevent herself from still sounding wooden, then felt guilty for the tiny wince her mother tried to hide.

"Then we'll see you tomorrow," Caroline said, forcing a friendly tone. "The doctors don't want him overdoing things."

"Of course."

After that they said their goodbyes but once in the car, Damien turned toward her, his eyes piercing. "Your father's still got a long way to go."

Gabrielle grimaced. "You don't have to remind me."

"Yes, I do. You seem to think if you ignore everything, then it will just sort itself out."

"Maybe it will," she said coolly.

"And maybe it won't," he snapped. "When your father struggles through all this to get better and finally comes home to find out his company has been decimated, will you tell him why there's nothing left? Or will you be back in Sydney and won't give a damn?"

She drew herself up straighter in the passenger seat. "Have you finished?"

"No I bloody well haven't."

She sucked in a sharp breath. "God, you're so like my father it isn't funny. The two of you could be twins."

A pulse began to beat in his cheekbone. "What are you talking about?"

Her heart squeezed tight. "You like things your own way, Damien. I won't marry you. I would end up a doormat who occasionally got taken out on special occasions. Just like my mother."

"No," he growled.

"You desire me, but once you get bored with me you'll move on to some other woman, and a marriage license won't stop you." She lifted her head high. "I want something better for myself than what my mother had with my father, and if I can't have a warm, loving marriage, then I don't want a poor imitation of one."

He went very still. "You don't know what I feel for you," he rasped.

"Exactly." She'd always known when he wanted her, but that hadn't been about his *feelings*. He'd kept his real feelings from showing.

"We'll talk later." He turned away and started the engine. "Let's get something to eat. It's way past lunchtime," he said, confirming what she'd just said about ignoring any feelings. "Then I need to go to my office for an hour or two."

She hadn't eaten a thing all day and she wasn't sure she could. Her appetite seemed to have disappeared. "I'd prefer to go talk to Keiran again."

His mouth tightened. "Best leave Keiran to think over things for the rest of the day. Otherwise we're going to antagonize him more, and right now that's probably not a good thing. I'll give James a call after we eat. He can keep an eye on things until tomorrow."

"Fine." She knew what he said made sense. But tomorrow, whether Keiran liked it or not…whether *Damien* liked it or not…she was going to take charge and damn the consequences.

Back at the apartment, while she made ham sandwiches for a late lunch, Damien got on the phone and arranged for a rental car for her use. Then they sat on the balcony and ate lunch.

"By the way," Damien said after a few minutes silence. "I have a dinner to attend tonight. I want you to come with me."

She placed her half-eaten sandwich back on her plate, a little hurt by his insensitivity. "Thanks but I'll pass. I don't feel like seeing people when my father's sick in hospital."

"It'll do you good to get out."

Her lips twisted in a grimace. "The last thing I feel like doing is attending some business dinner with a bunch of strangers."

"This isn't a business dinner. It's with friends."

She gave a choked laugh. "I didn't know you *had* any friends. Except *women* friends, of course."

He arched a brow. "You sound jealous."

"Only of their ability to put up with your delightful company," she said sweetly, ignoring the fact that he looked so handsome sitting there with the sun's shadow on his lean face.

He tilted his dark head, a slight smile on his lips. "Our marriage is going to be very interesting."

She stabbed him with a glare. "I am *not* marrying you, Damien."

The smile left his mouth. His gaze became shuttered. "Tonight's a good time to introduce you to them."

She felt as if she was going round and round in circles. "Damien, I—"

"Be ready by seven," he said, pushing his chair back and getting to his feet.

She looked up at him, suddenly tired of fighting him, knowing he wasn't about to give up. He'd probably even try to dress her himself if she wasn't ready. "Okay, fine. I'll go. But they're all probably a bunch of boring suits, anyway."

His eyes narrowed. "You might be surprised."

"About you? Never. I know the sort of man you are and the sort of friends you'll have."

A muscle began jumping in his cheek. "I'm glad you think you know me," he snapped, then strode back inside the apartment.

A few moments later she heard the front door close in a quiet, controlled manner. In a way she wished he'd slammed it instead.

A couple of hours later they drove up to a luxurious mansion along the waterfront at Cullen Bay. Gabrielle, dressed in a silky blue dress that had received an approving look from Damien, was proven right about his friends.

Yet wrong.

The house obviously belonged to moneyed people, but when she stepped inside the front door it was to find one other couple besides their hosts and a warm greeting that softened the hardness around her heart and made her feel very welcome. They were all very different from what she'd expected. And that added an insight into the man beside her that she would never have seen otherwise.

Danielle and Flynn Donovan owned the house, and

Kia and Brant Matthews were obviously close friends and frequent visitors. The women were gorgeous and friendly, the two men handsome and suave, but with a slight reserve that told Gabrielle they were the same breed as Damien. They didn't let down their guard easily.

Dinner was quite a lighthearted affair in a magnificent dining room that really showed off the house to perfection.

"This is such a lovely room," Gabrielle said to Danielle once they'd finished the first course and there was a lull in the conversation.

Danielle flushed, looking pleased. "Thank you. That's really nice of you to say so."

Something occurred to Gabrielle and her eyes widened. "I've just realized. *You* were the one who did Damien's apartment, weren't you?"

Danielle nodded with pleasure, though Gabrielle mentally acknowledged the mention of her knowing Damien's apartment had been noted by all of them.

"My wife is quite the decorator," Flynn said, sending his wife a loving look. It was a look that Gabrielle herself had hoped to receive one day from the man she loved.

At the thought, her gaze slid to Damien opposite her, and saw him watching her through half-closed lids. She wondered if Damien would ever be as relaxed as the men around their wives. He'd always seemed so alone.

Appearing nonchalant, she reached for her wineglass and took a sip, but her thoughts were far from casual. Damien had never sent her a loving look like the one Flynn had given his wife. Lustful yes, but not a warm look filled with respect.

Not that it mattered. She didn't plan on falling in love

again. Nor did she plan on marrying for a long time to come, despite what Damien said. For the moment she was just going to be one of those women whose dreams of being swept off her feet were just that—dreams.

"Gabrielle Kane?" the other woman, Kia, said with a slight frown on her beautiful forehead. "Your name seems familiar. Are you from Darwin?"

Gabrielle darted a look at Damien, but Kia's husband, Brant, pulled her gaze to him instead. "You're Russell Kane's daughter, aren't you?" he said, a curious gleam in his eyes that made her wonder what he knew about her. "You've been living interstate for the last couple of years."

She moistened her suddenly dry lips. "Yes, I have."

"Oh, that's right. Your father recently had a stroke," Kia said sympathetically. "I remember reading it in the newspapers now. I'm so sorry, Gabrielle. How is he?"

Gabrielle inclined her head in gratitude. "Thank you." Her voice broke a little, so she cleared her throat. "He's heavily sedated at the moment."

"But we're hoping he'll soon be on the mend," Damien added, his voice losing that steely edge, surprising Gabrielle, making her feel less alone in her fears.

"I'm so glad," Kia said with sincerity. She paused, her eyes a little surprised. "You know, Gabrielle. You're not like we expected."

Gabrielle grew a little wary, but wasn't sure why. "I'm not?"

Kia's lips curved into a smile. "You're much nicer." The other woman sent Damien an approving look. "I'm really glad Damien brought you here tonight."

Gabrielle let out a silent sigh of relief even as she refused to look at Damien. "So am I." And she meant it. She just wished it hadn't been because of Damien that she was here.

Then she realized the others were looking at her as if they knew there was more to her and Damien's relationship, but thankfully talk turned to general things while they worked their way through the rest of the meal.

Just as they were finishing dessert, the housekeeper, Louise, came into the room to tell both women that their babies were growing restless. Kia and Danielle instantly jumped up and so did their husbands, jokingly saying that they wanted to see their daughters, too.

Danielle went to leave the room, then stopped and frowned. She opened her mouth to speak but Damien cut her off, "Don't worry about us, Danielle. We'll be fine until you come back."

"Are you sure?"

Damien gave a slow smile. "What man in his right mind would complain about being left alone with such a beautiful woman?"

Danielle laughed. "Oh, you're such a smooth talker." She winked at Gabrielle. "Watch out for him, Gabrielle."

Gabrielle tried to smile but it felt forced. Her heart was thumping, and not just because she would be alone with Damien. She was so thankful the housekeeper hadn't brought either of those babies into the dining room. She wasn't sure she could bear it.

She waited until the others left the room, then put her

napkin on the table and stood. "I need some fresh air," she choked, hurrying toward the patio doors. They were closed to keep the room air-conditioned and she prayed they weren't locked. They weren't.

But as she stepped outside onto the well-lit terrace, the humidity that swamped her was as heavy as her heart. She stood there for a moment, letting it overwhelm her, welcoming the pain…the ache of loss.

"You don't like children?" Damien said from behind her, making her jump.

She schooled her features into a blank mask before slowly turning around. "What makes you say that?"

"Gut instinct. Most women usually fuss over babies and all that motherly stuff." His eyes pierced the distance between them. "You didn't."

She held his gaze. "Perhaps I have other things on my mind."

"Like what?"

"My father."

He inclined his head, conceding the point as he came toward her. "For your information, Kia's baby, Emma, is only a few weeks old. Danielle's little girl, Alexandra, is about nine months."

"I'm sure they're gorgeous," she said, her heart breaking even as she was surprised he knew the ages of his friends' children.

"They are."

She wanted to ask if he liked children. And if he ever planned on having another one day. Only, she couldn't say that. Not to the man who'd unknowingly fathered one child already. A child who had died.

She swallowed hard and tried not to let him see her anguish. "Your friends are really nice," she said, pushing aside her heartache.

"Not boring suits at all, eh?"

She winced. "No." She felt bad now for being so judgmental about them.

"Apology accepted."

Her eyes widened. "I didn't apologize."

"I know," he said with a slight smile as he came toward her.

She was suddenly too aware of how close he was. Quickly she turned away to look out over the lush landscape. "Um, this is a beautiful house. And this garden is just lovely."

Desperately she tried to concentrate on the beauty of the well-lit setting. A light breeze dipped palm fronds in the swimming pool, and flowers from the frangipani trees spread a blanket of white over a patch of lawn. Hibiscus provided splashes of red-orange color.

He put his hand on her arm and turned her back to him. Something deep kindled in his eyes. "Not as beautiful as you," he murmured, pulling her toward him.

Oh God. Five years ago she'd lacked the know-how to control her crazy feelings for him. Now she could feel the same craving for him gnawing beneath the surface.

"What do you want, Damien?" she said huskily, unable to stop herself from savoring the warm, male scent of him rising up in the pocket of air between them. At a subconscious level, it tantalized her senses and turned her legs to jelly.

His gaze dropped to her mouth. "You."

His head began to lower, and she unwillingly swayed toward him. Dear Lord. Suddenly five years was too long between kisses.

In the space of a heartbeat, he molded her mouth to the fullness of his own. Unable to ignore the taste of warm memories, she groaned and kissed him back, as a wonderful sensation quivered through her. Heat licked at her veins and she needed no further coaxing to let him venture into the hollows of her mouth while she clutched at his shoulders and let him intoxicate her.

Long moments later he broke off the kiss. She watched a pulse beat wildly in his throat, her mind staggered with incredulous wonder. She hadn't known it until now, but she'd missed this feeling of sharing and being one.

With him.

And then reality hit at the sound of the others coming back into the living room.

He stepped back and gestured for her to precede him through the patio doors. "After you," he murmured, the huskiness still lingering in his voice, affecting her, making her legs feel shaky as she hurried inside.

After that, the rest of the evening was nerve-racking for Gabrielle. Damien appeared to enjoy his friends' company, but whenever he looked at her, the desire in his eyes made her heart thud against her ribs.

Yet knowing she'd tapped a raw nerve back there on the patio gave her strength. She was glad their kiss had affected him as much as it had her. It made her feel not so needy. The downside was that it made her vulnerable. How could a woman *not* feel stirred knowing she'd touched a chord inside a man like Damien?

She breathed easier when he left the room to take a call on his cell phone, but his return sent a flutter of panic through her. There was an odd look in his eyes.

It was hard.

And determined.

She tried to ignore an uneasy feeling, but her heart jumped in her throat when not long after he suggested they leave. He didn't mention to the others she was staying with him. Not that it was anyone's business, and certainly Damien would never find the need to explain such a thing to anyone. Not even to his friends.

He didn't speak on the way home, either, but the tension increased within the confines of the car. Would he try to get her in bed? It certainly wouldn't worry him if he did, of that she was certain.

As soon as they stepped inside his apartment, the door to the spare bedroom appeared to be far too close for her liking. She darted a look at him beneath her lashes and saw a muscle ticking in his jaw. Her stomach tied itself in knots.

"Don't worry. I'm not going to seduce you," he mocked, striding over to the bar.

Her brows rose. "You're not?"

"Not yet anyway." He poured himself a small amount of scotch.

She moistened her lips, all at once certain there was something else going on here. "How…generous of you."

There was a moment's pause, then, "I've decided to wait until our marriage."

Frustration clawed through her. "Damien, will you please stop—"

"Tomorrow."

The air whooshed out of her lungs. "Wh-what?"

He took a swallow of his drink. "We're getting married tomorrow, Gabrielle, like it or not."

She gasped. "Look, I told you—"

"Keiran just lost a three-million-dollar contract."

Her head reeled back. "Say that again."

"That phone call I took was from James. Keiran lost a deal your father had been working on for the past year." He paused as he slammed the glass down on top of the bar. "Now. Don't you think it's time we got married?"

Five

The next afternoon Gabrielle married Damien in a simple ceremony held in his apartment, and Damien signed over eleven percent of Kane Property and Finance Group shares to her.

The only "family" Damien wanted to invite were his two best friends and their wives, and his attorney. No one else knew. Everything had to be kept secret so that Keiran wouldn't get wind of the marriage and do something underhanded to prevent it, if indeed there was anything he *could* do about it.

As for her parents, Damien suggested it was best not to tell them about the wedding until afterward. The excitement might not be good for her father, and her mother might let something slip to Keiran, especially since Damien had said later that Caroline had no idea about the shares.

Still, it had been hard for Gabrielle to visit her parents earlier that morning and act as if nothing momentous was about to happen. Thankfully, her father had been sleeping and her mother had asked Gabrielle to sit with him while she went home to shower and change. It had been a blessed relief not to have to put on a brave face. Nor was Gabrielle sure she wouldn't have begged her mother to stop her from doing a crazy thing like getting married two days after returning home.

And it *was* a crazy thing to do, she kept thinking when Kia and Danielle arrived carrying a gorgeous white sheath of a dress with a miniveil, and a posy of glorious miniature yellow roses. Suitably horrified at the speed Damien had arranged everything, they gave him a scolding about rushing the bride off her feet, yet they all knew why.

Thank goodness she didn't have to play the blushing bride in front of everyone, Gabrielle told herself while she was dressing, with Kia and Danielle sympathizing over her predicament in the background. Brant and Flynn's attitude was that Damien was doing the right thing, which made all three women smile wryly at each other in a moment of bonding.

Of course, once the ceremony was over and she stood next to the ladies beside a table covered with scrumptious food, she was on autopilot as she sipped at her champagne. The men had gone out on the balcony on the pretext of admiring the panoramic ocean view, but were deep in discussion instead.

"You know something, Gabrielle," Kia said. "Damien reminds me so much of Brant and Flynn. Handsome. Gorgeous. And wonderful husbands once you get past the wall of detachment that's inherent in men like them."

Sudden despair wrapped around Gabrielle's heart. She was sure Damien would be just like her father. And she would turn out just like her mother.

"Good heavens, your hands are shaking," Kia exclaimed in a sympathetic tone. She squeezed Gabrielle's arm. "Honey, we understand. Danielle and I felt the same way about our guys when we first met them."

Danielle nodded in agreement. "That's right. And one day we'll tell you all about it, but not now. It would take too long to explain why Flynn thought I was after his money," she said with rueful smile. "But I do want to say one thing—trust that it will work out for the two of you."

Gabrielle appreciated their kindness, but there was so much that they didn't realize. For one thing these women didn't know about her and Damien's past affair. Nor about her miscarriage—the one Damien didn't know about, either.

Just then she looked up and saw the three men coming back inside the apartment through the sliding glass doors. Damien looked magnificent in a dark suit and white shirt and was grinning at something one of the others had said. It was a striking smile that curled her toes and sent her heart thudding against her ribs.

And then he saw her staring at him and he paused briefly, before his mouth tilted in a sardonic grin. "I hope you ladies aren't plying my new bride with alcohol," he said, walking toward them.

Kia gave a light laugh. "Of course we are."

"I have something much better." He nodded at the waiter, who proceeded to hand out fresh glasses of champagne.

Despite his relaxed air, those piercing eyes studied her thoughtfully for a moment, giving nothing away. And then she saw a hint of satisfaction lurking at the back of them, and fear rippled through her. Fear, not of Damien himself, but of where all this was leading. He may not have planned to marry her when he'd brought her back from Sydney, but he certainly intended to profit from all this…in more ways than one.

He held up his glass. "A toast. To my new wife."

From somewhere deep inside her, she managed to raise her own glass and smile right back at him. "And here's to my old husband."

That evening, alone with Damien on his luxury yacht, Gabrielle ignored the man beside her and purposely focused her gaze on Darwin Harbor. In the remaining light, she watched as other boats sailed past them over the deep, calm water, the sound of laughter and clinking glasses sometimes drifting through the air, early evening being all about relaxing and having fun.

Not for them, of course. She didn't want to be here. It was under duress and Damien knew it. So she wasn't feeling particularly friendly toward him right now.

Okay, so he'd looked handsome and virile as he'd motored the vessel out himself, then dropped anchor, the cream polo shirt enhancing his well-built body as he'd moved, the black trousers molding perfectly to his long legs.

She'd always loved looking at his profile, and he looked even more attractive this evening with the water reflecting on his face. There was something very potent about the picture he made, and she felt a tremor inside knowing she was now married to him.

Her husband.

All at once he turned his head toward her. His moss-green eyes stared across the table and into her own with a burning intensity. "You were a beautiful bride."

She realized she was gripping her wineglass so tight she might break it. She forced her fingers to relax. "Thank you."

"You won my friends over well and truly," he added.

She grimaced. They both knew Brant and Flynn approved because they thought she was doing the right thing for the business. "I'm sure Kia and Danielle feel a certain…empathy for me."

His slight smile noted her comment. "The girls might be able to relate, but you can't discount the fact they are very happily married."

She met his gaze levelly. "They're in love, Damien. We're not."

He didn't miss a beat. "You're right. Here's to *not* being in love," he drawled, lifting his glass of white wine.

Five years ago she would have been devastated by his words, but she knew she was beyond that now.

She raised her glass and clinked it against his. "That's a toast I can relate to."

"And to us," he added.

She pulled the glass back. "There's no such thing as 'us,' Damien. There's you. And there's me. Two separate entities."

"Not after tonight."

The pit of her stomach began to churn. "I could scream, you know."

"So could I."

The comment was so unexpected that her lips twitched.

"Is that a smile I see?" he teased, sounding as if he was truly amused. It was a glimpse of how it could have been if only…

She remembered what their marriage was about. "No," she said, not looking at him, instead looking everywhere *but* at him. "I have nothing to smile about."

A moment passed by. "You're my wife now," he said with quiet emphasis. "Accept it."

She lifted her chin as she looked at him. "I guess I should be honored to be Mrs. Damien Trent?" she said sarcastically, even as she suppressed a tingle at her new name.

"Naturally."

She made a choking sound. "Your arrogance astounds me," she said, and caught a look of surprise on his face that in turn surprised *her*. He really had no idea his words had come across as arrogant. He really did believe she should be honored to marry him.

As if!

No way would she be grateful to a man who forced her into… She winced inwardly. He hadn't forced her into anything. Yes, he'd married her for his own purposes. And yes, he'd married her for her father's sake—but for an honorable reason.

She hadn't quite thought about it in this light before, but by marrying her today he was showing what kind of man he was—an honorable one. He must have had a good upbringing.

Suddenly she realized, Damien hadn't mentioned his parents today, not once. And she'd been too preoccupied and busy to ask the question.

Now she had the time. "Why didn't you invite your parents to the wedding, Damien?"

He tensed. "It would be a bit hard. They're dead," he said in a clipped tone that didn't ask for sympathy and would accept none.

A wave of compassion swept over her. And as strange as it seemed, she felt a little sad that she'd never get to meet the parents of this man. Five years ago they'd been on a round-the-world cruise, though she suspected he wouldn't have introduced her, anyway. About the only other thing she knew about him was that he didn't have any brothers or sisters, and even getting that out of him had been like asking for state secrets.

"What happened?" she asked sympathetically.

The line of his mouth flattened. "My father picked up some sort of bug during their cruise. It killed him before he could get proper medical attention."

Her eyes widened. "Oh my God. That's dreadful. Your poor mother. Did she—"

"She died two years ago."

She listened in dismay. "I'm so sorry, Damien."

"Thanks," he said, looking out to sea, making her

think he had hidden depths she was only now beginning to notice.

"So you're all alone in the world?" she said, trying to find what made this man tick.

He looked at her with eyes turned hooded and dark, a sure sign she'd touched a nerve. "If you want to think of it that way, yes." Then as if he'd had enough talking, he rose up from his chair like some god ready to sacrifice a virgin. If she'd had time she would have laughed at the thought, but her heart was jumping inside her chest as he came around the table toward her.

"Wh-what are you doing?"

He stopped in front of her, took the glass out of her hand, and pulled her to her feet, his hands circling her waist. "What do you think I'm doing?"

"No, Damien."

Something lazily seductive seeped into his eyes. "Yes, Gabrielle."

"Damien, I'm not ready—"

"I'm five years ready."

She blinked. "Are you saying…you've been celibate for five years?"

He snorted. "I'm a man, not a saint."

Of course. How silly of her. "Then what did—"

"Shhhhhh." He lowered his head and kissed her. She inhaled sharply and his tongue swept into her mouth, sweeping aside her objections like he did with everything else.

The sheer passion behind it…the possessiveness in it…took her breath away. She melted into him with a low moan, a part of her dismayed at how easily she weakened, another part gloriously alive, reveling in the feel of his lips against hers.

And with each passing moment those firm, manly lips hardened with increasing hunger, growing more urgent and demanding. She returned his kiss, her heartbeat throbbing in her ears, his scent hugging her lungs until all she knew was him.

He lifted his mouth and sent her a heated look, and a private message passed between them. He, too, remembered how it had been. A delicious shudder swept over her. She could almost taste the saltiness of his skin and feel the heat of his body as they lay entwined in bed together.

"It's time, Gabrielle."

"Time?" she asked breathlessly, delaying the inevitable, though she wasn't sure why now.

"For our bodies to do the talking."

Before she could say anything…or *do* anything except admit to herself she had a need for him…he put her hand in his and drew her along behind him, down the stairs to the cabin below.

She allowed him to lead her, all at once feeling this was meant to be. She could no more stop this from happening than stop the tide from turning. She didn't *want* to stop it now. Deep down she'd known that all along.

And then they were beside the bed and Damien stood looking at her, the lights from the deck filtering in through the windows, giving their world a pearly glow.

A sense of intimacy swirled around them as his fingers feathered up her arm, igniting little sparks where they touched her skin…up over the curve of her shoulder…along her collarbone…under her hair at her nape, admiring the blond strands cascading over his fingers.

"My blond beauty," he murmured, and brought her mouth to his once more, this time capturing it in a slow and sensuous possession.

She dissolved against him, loving the way his sinewy body embraced hers, his needing her as much as she needed him. And she was lost. As lost as any woman had a right to be when in the arms of a man she'd once loved.

Moments crept by before he eased away from mouth. "It's been a long time for us," he said, placing his lips against the column of her throat.

Ahh! She tingled at his touch, every pore in her body recognizing him, acknowledging him. It was five years since he'd made love to her like this. In her dreams it had sometimes seemed like yesterday. In her nightmares it had been forever.

"Say it, Gabrielle. Say you missed this, too."

She stretched her neck back allowing him access to the base of her throat. "Yes," she whispered. "I missed this."

His grunt of approval made her head spin as his hands slipped around to her back and slowly lowered the zip of her dress. The material fell to her waist and she stood in her lacy black bra, her nipples swelling in anticipation, her pulse rioting with need. She wanted to feel his mouth against her breasts.

"Mine," he said, his voice rough with need, arching her up for his indulgence, his eyes darkening as he took what was so willingly offered.

"Yes," she murmured, then gasped at the touch of his lips closing around a nipple.

He sucked hard, the lace emphasizing the abrasive action of his tongue, and she clutched at his shoulders as he moved to the other breast and repeated the rhythm, creating wonderful little bursts of ecstasy within the very core of her.

Then he undid her bra and it fell to the floor. Her breasts spilled into his hands and she moaned aloud with sheer pleasure when he began to fondle them. Oh my, did he know what he was doing to her?

Then those hands…those superb male hands…slipped over her rib cage, his firm fingers kneading her skin. Her dress began to slip downward, over her hips, her stomach…and all at once she was conscious of what he would find, and she stiffened, preparing herself for the moment he felt her scar. It didn't take long.

His fingers stopped on the flat skin of her stomach. "What the hell!" He put her away from him, twisting her toward the light shining in through the window to get a better look.

A flush seared her cheeks. "I'm sorry, I—"

"What happened?" he demanded, holding her hips firm, a muscle jerking in his cheek, an angry look exploding in his eyes. Angry and…pained.

She tried to pull away but he wouldn't let her. "A car accident. I know it looks horrible but—"

"No," he growled. "It doesn't." And he fell on one knee to place his lips against the two-inch jagged scar radiating downward from her belly button.

She shuddered helplessly. Of all the things she expected, it wasn't that he would touch her with such sensitivity. In a strange way it made her proud of him. Proud to be his woman, if only in a physical way.

"Thank you," she said softly.

"No need," he muttered, and placed his lips against her scar one more time. Then his hands left her hips and cupped her bottom, pulling her forward and pressing his face against the very intimate part of her.

Her heart stopped for a long moment as he held her like that, as if discovering her scent again and reveling in it. She grasped his shoulders before her legs buckled beneath her.

He took a deep breath and moved back to slowly peel her panties down her legs. Leaning on him, she stepped out of them, but he stayed where he was, just looking at her.

Suddenly she felt self-conscious. Damien had been her only lover. And it had been five years since he'd seen her naked body like this. She went to cover herself, but he made a sound low in his throat and pushed her hands away, then began kissing his way upward, his lips like silk along her thighs, over the blond curls hiding her femininity, skimming up over the sensitized skin of her breasts before anointing each nipple again, then moving up further and settling on her mouth.

His tongue danced with hers as he pulled her against him, his hardened body straining the material of his pants, sending a flash of heat through her. She was ready for him. More than ready.

"I want to feel you against me," he rasped, and stepped back, stripping the clothes from his body so fast he made her head spin. She wanted to say "take your time, let me look," but a more-eager part of her had a need low in her stomach at the sight of his obvious arousal.

He sank down on the bed behind him, drawing her close, positioning her so she stood between his legs. His mouth began to tease her nipples and she closed her eyes, welcoming his touch, winding her fingers through his hair, holding his head tight between her hands.

Just when she thought she could no longer stand, when a cry of pleasure was about to burst from her lips, he lay back on the bed and slowly stretched her out alongside him, so they were facing each other.

She moaned, and buried her face against his throat, savoring the touch of every inch of masculine skin lining hers. Dear heaven, she only had to guide him inside her and they would be one.

For several long seconds they lay there, as if he too, were soaking up the feel of skin against skin, the rocking of the boat giving a lulling sensation to their lovemaking.

Then he leaned up on his elbow and slowly began to trace a fingertip over the top of her breasts, his finger scorching everywhere he touched, down her cleavage pressed tight by the angle of her body.

"Look," he ordered thickly, his gaze descending between them. Her limbs quivered as she looked down to where their bodies touched. All the way down.

Man against woman.

"A perfect fit," he said, his eyes now locked on hers.

She swallowed tremulously. "Yes," she said, growing warm and welcoming, a wantonness forming in her lower limbs.

All at once he rose up over her toward the bedside table and took a condom out of the top drawer. "Here," he said, handing it to her, a pulse beating in his neck.

The breath stalled in her throat. "Oh but—"

"You want me to wear it, don't you?" he challenged in a raw mutter.

She moistened her lips. She couldn't think. Yes. No. "Um...yes."

"Then put it on me," he rasped with his usual arrogance, only she couldn't seem to respond in kind. Perhaps because she could see her effect on him. He couldn't hide how he was feeling right now; it was an empowering thought.

She tried to open the small foil package but her fingers shook and she dropped it. Giving her a look that said he was pleased she *wasn't* an expert in this, he took it and ripped it open with his teeth, then held it out to her.

But she didn't take it just yet. Swallowing hard, she looked down at him and felt a sizzle run through her. She had wanted to touch him before, and now she would.

She reached out and slid her hand around his erection, hearing a groan rise up from his throat, making the breath hitch in her throat. His skin felt warm under her palms. Warm and vital and so very Damien.

Without warning he muttered, "No more," then put his hand over hers and released her fingers from around him. In the blink of an eye, he rolled the condom on himself, moved her back against the bed, then nudged her thighs until she opened herself to him.

Only, he didn't enter her just then. He waited, looking

down at her with darkened eyes, the cords in his neck straining as he held his body above her…waiting…

"Come into me, Damien," she said, sliding her palm over his chest.

And that was enough. On a groan, he pushed himself into her wet warmth.

Slowly.

Exquisitely.

Filling her with a sense of completeness.

Even five years ago their lovemaking hadn't been as rich as this. It was much richer now in intensity, in depth, in experience.

And then he kissed her deeply as he moved erotically in and out. She loved the way he explored her inner womanhood with a thoroughness and pleasure that stamped her as his own, leaving no part of her untouched.

She moaned and inched toward the peak of desire. Unable to hold out against such an onslaught, she shut her eyes giddily. And she told herself to wait. That she wanted it to last forever. But her body wasn't about to stop from rejoicing in their mating.

She escalated higher and higher, with nothing to hold on to except this man within her. "Damien, please… Damien, I need you…Damien…"

"Gabi," he rasped, and she felt him pulsing into her, her own femininity cupping him tight in her climax, welcoming his sheathed essence.

A long moment later she was left with one thought and one thought only. The last time they'd made love he'd called her Gabi. And he'd been inside her back then, too.

* * *

The next morning Damien kept his eyes closed as he enjoyed the slight rocking of the boat and inhaled the scent of Gabrielle in the tropical air. It woke his body, arousing him with the pleasure of the night.

Many pleasures of the night.

He rolled on his side and reached for her, but his hand found a cool cotton sheet instead of a warm body. His eyes opened. She was probably in the bathroom. Or making coffee in the galley.

He listened for any sound of her. All was quiet. He sniffed the air and waited. Any minute now the aromatic smell of coffee would tantalize his nostrils. When nothing happened, he eased into a sitting position and looked around the cabin. Unless she'd jumped overboard, she'd still have to be on the yacht.

His heart started to thump. Or perhaps she'd taken the dingy. If she had, he'd kill her, he decided, throwing back the sheet, his gut knotting as he pulled on his trousers. He didn't bother about a shirt as he took the stairs two at a time.

When he found her on the top deck, it took a moment to steady his heartbeat. Then he strode toward her and hauled her into his arms.

"Damien, what the—"

He dropped a fierce kiss on her lips. It was supposed to be an angry kiss for being foolish enough to leave him. Only, after a moment or two, with her palms flattened on his bare chest, he found he was more hungry for her than angry, more searching than punishing. He wanted her to know how waking up this morning without her had felt. It had been the same feeling he'd experienced five years ago.

He broke off the kiss and muttered, "There's no escape."

She looked confused. "I wasn't trying to escape."

Okay, he'd panicked. He wouldn't do it again. "Tell me about the car accident."

Her face closed up and she stepped out of his arms and went to sit down on a seat. "Why? Am I imperfect now, Damien?"

"No." She was too damn perfect to look at. That was the problem. He winced inwardly. No, he didn't quite mean that. Gabrielle wasn't just about her looks.

She leaned back and stared up at him, gorgeous in white pants and a lime-green top. "What do you want to know?"

"How it happened. *When* did it happen. Everything."

Her lips, still slightly swollen from his kiss, curved in a wry smile. "You don't ask for much, do you?"

He didn't find it remotely funny. "I'm telling, not asking."

Her eyes clouded over. "Yes, that's more your style."

"Gabrielle, you're procrastinating." His eyes narrowed. "What are you hiding?"

She looked startled. "Nothing," she said, much too fast for his liking. She moistened her delicious mouth. "Er…it happened a few months after I went to Sydney. I was a passenger in a car with one of Eileen's daughters, Lara. This drunken idiot came out of nowhere and his car hit the front passenger side and some metal buckled and cut me."

"Sweet Jesus!" The thought of it made him taste bile.

All at once she was looking at him as if realizing his shock. "Damien, I'm fine," she said gently.

Her tone didn't soothe him. He felt savage. Like he wanted to commit murder. "What happened to this idiot? He'd better be in jail."

"I don't know. I was in hospital for a few days, then I was too busy getting back on my feet."

"If I'd known…" he growled, a burning sensation in his throat. "If Russell had known…"

An uneasy look entered her eyes. "Thankfully neither of you did." As quickly, she drew herself up, a certain coolness taking over. "And thankfully neither of you had a say in my life after that." She paused for effect. "I just wish you didn't have a say now."

The muscles at the back of his neck tensed. "You're married to me, Gabrielle. From here on in, whatever happens, I want to know about it."

Her eyes flashed with cynicism. "It didn't take long for you to start trying to control me."

He stared hard at her. She'd taken that the wrong way. He was concerned for her, not controlling. He wanted to make sure she'd didn't get hurt again. God, he hated thinking about her trapped in a car. About her lying in hospital.

His jaw clenched. But if she preferred to think the worst of his motives, then let her. He wasn't explaining himself to anyone.

He made a move toward the stairs. "Get your things together. We're going back to shore."

Six

When they arrived back at the apartment, Gabrielle half expected Damien to carry her off to bed, and firmly squashed a sense of disappointment when he strode straight over to the dining table and started sorting through his briefcase.

"You're working *now?*" she asked, then realized how that sounded. "I mean, aren't we going to see my parents?"

He glanced at his Rolex, his attitude telling her he was a busy man. "I've got a couple of calls to make, then we'll go break the news of our marriage to your mother. We'll leave it up to Caroline to decide whether to tell Russell yet or not."

Gabrielle swallowed, feeling guilty. In a way she didn't really feel she *should* feel too guilty about it. Not after everything her parents had put her through. Yet she did.

"And by the way," he added. "I've ordered a Porsche to replace the rental car."

Gabrielle groaned, feeling swallowed up by him. "You did?"

"And I've told your ex-boss, Eileen, we were getting married."

Her eyes widened in dismay. "You didn't!" Now *this* she did feel guilty over.

"I had to give her some reason why I was having your things sent up here."

She couldn't believe he'd done all this without asking her. "You really are a piece of work, aren't you?" she snapped, then spun toward the spare bedroom, intending to use the phone in there. "I'd better phone her on the other extension and explain." Eileen had been so good to her and would be disappointed not to have been invited to the wedding.

"Gabrielle?"

She stopped at the bedroom door. "What?"

"You're in the master bedroom now," he drawled, nodding his head at the other bedroom door. "With me."

A tremor of desire quaked through her body. "*Master bedroom*?" she scoffed. "Oh, goodie. I can sit at your feet and feed you grapes all day."

His expression relaxed into a smile, and it was devastating. "I can't see you being part of a harem."

"I'm amazed you appreciate that."

His eyes dropped to her breasts. "Oh, I appreciate you just fine, Gabrielle."

She moved slightly to cover her tingling nipples beneath her lime-green top. "Don't you have some calls to make?" she pointed out sourly, intending to shower and change out of her white slacks and into something more suitable for the office, just as soon as she spoke to Eileen.

His lips curled faintly upward. "They'll be brief."

"Well, *I* could be a while," she said, letting him know he'd caused problems and now she had to clean up his mess.

He ignored that. "I'll come get you when you're ready."

"So you have X-ray vision and can see through walls now?" she derided. "I think you've been eating too many carrots."

"No, grapes," he mocked, then strode out onto the balcony, already pressing the numbers on his cell phone, already forgetting her.

She didn't smile, though she secretly appreciated the smart comment. And she was still appreciating it after talking to Eileen, and then an hour later when they took her mother aside and told her the news. Gabrielle had already insisted that she wanted to be the one to tell her mother, though how on earth did she explain without telling her the true reason?

She didn't expect Caroline to burst into tears. "Mum, I'm sorry but it was a spur-of-the-moment thing."

Caroline dabbed at her eyes with a tissue. "But I'm your mother, Gabrielle. I would have liked to be at my only child's wedding."

Damien put his arm around Gabrielle's shoulders and pulled her close. "Caroline, we knew you'd be torn about leaving Russell's side, so we decided it was best we didn't tell you until it was over."

She still looked hurt. "But couldn't you both have waited until Russell was better?"

"I'm sorry, no," Damien said quietly but firmly. "I wanted Gabrielle to marry me and I couldn't wait a moment longer for her." He looked down at Gabrielle with a warm look in his eyes that totally shook her, then he squeezed her shoulder, urging her to back him up, making her realize it was all a front.

"Yes, that's right," Gabrielle confirmed. "We just couldn't wait. I'm sorry," she said, feeling really bad now. She knew her parents loved her. She didn't like causing them pain, despite how much they'd caused her.

Caroline sniffed. "You must love each other very much," she said, relenting.

"We do," Damien said without hesitation, and for a split second Gabrielle actually thought he meant it. Her heart gave a thud, then settled down to reality.

"Russell will be pleased," Caroline said. A frown marred her forehead. "But perhaps we shouldn't tell him until I speak to his doctor?"

"Good idea," Damien said. "And look, I know Russell's been too sick to have visitors, but don't let Keiran in to see him just yet. He might slip up and give it away about our marriage, and I'd hate to set Russell back because he received a shock."

She nodded even as she looked startled. "Keiran knows about your marriage?"

"Not yet. We're on our way to the office soon to tell him."

"Oh, good. He'll be so surprised. And delighted, too, no doubt. He's taken on a big responsibility trying to fill

Russell's shoes, always phoning me and checking to see how your father is doing. He's been such a comfort." She smiled warmly. "As you both have."

"Don't worry, Caroline," Damien said. "We intend to help him as much as we can."

Her mother's brow rose. "We?"

Gabrielle knew she had to tell her mother their plans. "Mum, Damien's going to help me run the company until Dad gets better."

Her mother's face lit up. "Really?"

"Yes." Deliberately she didn't mention Keiran. If her mother asked, she would say he intended to help out in another capacity at the office.

"That's wonderful, darling. I'm so proud of you." She glanced at Damien. "Russell always thought of you as a son, Damien. I'm sure he'll be thrilled about this."

Damien cleared his throat. "He's been like a father to me, too, Caroline," he said, sounding gruff.

Caroline gave a light laugh. "Good heavens, I now have a son-in-law. Who would've believed it?" She winked at Gabrielle. "And maybe one day I'll be a grandma?" she teased, a sudden speculative light in her eyes.

Gabrielle stiffened, but she was sure only Damien felt it. "Not yet, Mum. I have too much to do to help Dad first."

Caroline looked only slightly disappointed. "That's okay, darling. But I look forward to the day when you're ready to give me a little grandbaby."

Gabrielle swallowed hard. She wasn't sure that day would ever come again.

As if Damien knew she was uneasy, he changed the subject. "How about when Russell's better we have another ceremony? A big event with lots of family and friends. What do you think, Caroline? Would you and Russell like that?"

Caroline's eyes lit up. "Oh yes, that would be wonderful." Then the light in her eyes dimmed. "Of course, I'm not sure where I'll be once Russell gets better…"

Gabrielle's heart thudded to a halt. "Mum?"

Caroline patted her hand. "Darling, I came back because I love your father and he's sick, but I don't know whether he still loves me."

Gabrielle was horrified. She'd thought her parents were back together. "Mum, of course he does."

Caroline frowned. "To be honest, I'm not sure." Then her mother fluttered a dismissive hand. "But this is about you and Damien, not me and Russell. And I promise that no matter where I am I'll come back for another ceremony."

Gabrielle was having trouble trying to come to terms with her mother's admission that she hadn't resumed her marriage, so she was thankful when Damien stepped in and suggested they leave.

"Don't let the comment about grandchildren worry you," he said on the way out of the hospital. "Your mother's just doing some wishful thinking. It's only natural."

Somehow she found the strength to pretend she didn't care that her parents should have already been grandparents. If only…

No!

Instead, she shot Damien a glare. "Did you know they weren't actually back together?"

"Yes," he said, opening the car door for her.

"What! You told me—"

"That your mother had come home because of your father's stroke. She did."

"But—"

"Let them work it out themselves. We have other things to worry about right now." He took her elbow and guided her onto the passenger seat. "Keiran being one of them. He's bound to be difficult."

The thought of facing Keiran kept her quiet as Damien closed the door and came around the other side of the BMW. A short while later they entered her father's office to find her cousin again behind the desk, looking so self-satisfied she wanted to wipe that look right off his face. Thank goodness she'd dressed in a short black skirt and cream silk blouse that looked very businesslike.

"Keiran," she said, walking over to the chair in front of the desk and taking a seat as Damien went to stand by the window. "Do you realize you lost the company a three-million-dollar contract?"

Keiran suddenly looked wary. "They wanted more than we could give. We don't have the resources for what they wanted."

"No," she snapped. "My father would have bent over backward to find a way to keep that contract."

Keiran glared at her defiantly. "I did all I could."

"I'm sure you did. But this company isn't only about you and what *you* can and can't do, Keiran. It's about being a business. About keeping people in jobs."

Keiran stiffened. "Don't come in here and start

preaching to me on how to run things, Gabrielle. I'm in charge now and there's nothing you can do about it."

"Correction. You *were* in charge."

He rolled his eyes. "Don't start that again. You and Damien are—"

"Married."

He flinched, then quickly recovered. "So?"

She leaned forward and slapped a copy of the marriage certificate and the document transferring the shares on the desk. "We're married. We were married yesterday. And Damien's given me eleven percent of his shares as a wedding present," she said, enjoying dropping that bombshell. She made a point of standing up. "So thank you for holding the fort, but I'll take over now."

"Like hell you will," Keiran snapped, his face turning an ugly red.

"Gabrielle has every right to be here," Damien pointed out curtly.

The other man swore. "You won't get me out that easily."

Damien's brow rose. "Really?"

Keiran jumped to his feet. "Oh, you both think you're clever, don't you?" He snatched the copied certificates and shoved them in his jacket pocket as he strode around the desk. "I'm going to see my lawyer."

"Feel free," Damien said in a cool tone. "And Keiran?"

Keiran stopped on his way to the door. "What?" he snarled.

"Make sure you go back to your own office next time."

The door slammed shut behind him.

Gabrielle's heart tried to settle. "That went well," she half joked.

"Better than expected," Damien returned with a small smile that made her heart beat faster despite the tenseness of the situation with Keiran.

Ignoring the effect he had on her, she got to her feet and walked around the large desk. For a moment she stood, looking over the spacious office, suddenly feeling overwhelmed.

She was in charge.

She had business decisions to make.

Employees to look after.

"Oh God. What was I thinking, Damien? Keiran was right. I don't know how to run a business, let alone a big company like—"

"But *I* do. And I'll help you all the way," he reminded her.

She nodded and sat in her father's chair. She should have felt intimidated even further, but all at once just sitting where her father had sat every day for years, knowing he was in hospital and needed her help, gave her strength.

She took a deep breath. "Thanks. Now where do we start?"

A hint of admiration entered his eyes, warming her. "First order of the day, I need to go see a few people and try to win back that lost contract."

She frowned. "Do you think you can?"

He gave her a wry look. "Do you doubt it?"

She had to smile. "No."

He gave a slight smile in return, and something sizzled in the air between them.

Then he stepped toward the door. "I'd better go see these people and repair the damage."

She watched him walk away, the huskiness in his voice making her pulse race through her veins.

Then all at once he stopped to look back at her. "Don't forget that we need to act like a loving couple, otherwise it could undermine confidence in the company."

His words put everything back into perspective. Her lips twisted. "I'm not likely to forget it," she said with a touch of sarcasm, and received a sharp look in reply. He had no idea how much he sounded like her father.

It was seven-thirty before Damien walked into his apartment that evening, his body impatient as he waited to see Gabrielle again. They'd had a productive day, first with a promise from their previous clients to revisit the contract, and next with the meeting of department heads, who'd shown them total support. Then he'd dropped Gabrielle off here before going back to his own office to tidy up a few loose ends.

And now soft music greeted him. He dropped his briefcase on the sofa just as he heard a noise from the kitchen. He strode toward the sound, the blood beginning to pound through his veins. He and Gabrielle had acted like a newly married couple today at the office, though neither of them had gone overboard. Just a slight touch of their hands. A soft look at each other. A smiling agreement to a work decision.

Tonight he wanted more of her attention.

She was a sight for sore eyes, he mused, as he stood in the doorway watching her sprinkle chocolate pieces over some sort of dessert topped with cream. She was concentrating so hard, the tip of her tongue appeared, as if in temptation. A tip that had ran itself around his mouth last night while making love.

He groaned to himself as his gaze slid over her. She'd changed into a long, summery, floral dress that flared around her slim calves. Below it she was barefoot, her sandals having been kicked to the side as if she'd flung them off in a moment of passion.

"Damien!" Gabrielle said, as she'd turned and saw him in the doorway. "I didn't see you there."

"I know," he muttered, having trouble dragging his eyes away from those pink toenails and slender arches.

She seemed to realize he was mesmerized by her bare feet. A blush stole into her cheeks and she quickly stopped what she was doing and went to step into her shoes. "My feet were hot and the floor was cool and—"

"Leave them off."

She blinked. "Wh-what?"

"I like seeing you barefoot."

For the space of a heartbeat he thought she was going to comply. Then she continued putting her sandals on. "No, that's okay. My feet are cold now anyway."

"Then you must be the only person in Darwin with cold feet," he teased.

She ignored that. "It's the air-conditioning. I turned it up," she said, hurrying to the refrigerator with the bowl of dessert, looking delightfully flustered.

Then he watched her go over to the wall oven and turn on the inside light to check the casserole. His brows drew together. "I don't expect you to come home from the office and make dinner, you know. That's why I have a housekeeper."

"I know, but I can put a casserole in the oven. And it didn't take much to whip up dessert." She gave a tiny pause. "As a thank-you for all you did today."

Something inside his chest tilted and suddenly he wanted to kiss her. "You made dessert for me?"

"Yes." She spun away and went to the sink, but her voice held a husky tone. "Perhaps you'd better go shower?"

He loosened his tie. "Want to join me?"

She looked over her shoulder at him. "And ruin dinner?" she said dryly, but her cheeks turned rosy.

"We wouldn't want that," he mocked, deciding he would make her pay for that remark later. He turned and walked away.

In the bedroom, a strange comfort swelled inside his chest when he saw that she'd hung her clothes in the walk-in wardrobe next to his. Then he entered the bathroom and saw her makeup and hairbrush on the counter. It was such a feminine sight that he smiled to himself as he showered. It was an odd feeling sharing his private space with a woman.

Permanently.

Fifteen minutes later they sat at the dining table. "Did you phone the hospital?" he asked as he spooned beef casserole onto his plate.

She swallowed her mouthful of food then nodded. "Dad was asleep, but they're pleased with his progress. Mum said that if she hires a nurse, they might let him go home next week"

"Good." He placed the spoon back in the dish and reached for the scalloped potatoes. "Tell me. Did you ever finish your degree?"

Her fork suspended in midair, wariness filled her eyes. "Er…no."

"So you've given up your dream?"

Her expression clouded. "What dream?"

"I remember how you wanted to become a dietician. You said you wanted to help children learn to eat healthily so they'd grow to be healthy adults."

She shrugged. "Maybe one day I'll return to it."

He frowned with the feeling that she wasn't being as offhand as she pretended, but left it at that. He hated to see anyone give up on their dreams but now was not the time to sort this out. They had too many other things to settle first.

After that, they ate without talking. The casserole was delicious, and so was the chocolate mousse topped with whipped cream she'd made for dessert.

"Leave it," he said when she went to tidy up.

She grimaced. "I can't leave all these dirty dishes for your housekeeper."

One eyebrow slanted. "That's why I employ her. If you do her job, she won't have one." He must remember to tell Lila about his new change in circumstances, though she'd probably guessed something was going on, with Gabrielle's things in his bedroom, he mused.

Gabrielle's lips quirked. "That's true. But let me just put the leftovers away and the dirty dishes in the dishwasher. We can't leave this sitting here all night."

"Fine. I'll help you." He reached for the empty dishes.

She blinked in surprise. "You will?"

"Of course. I don't usually leave a mess, either."

She relaxed into a smile. "So you're domesticated?" she joked as she started carrying some of the plates back to the kitchen.

He looked at those lips and wanted to kiss the smile right off them. "Sometimes," he drawled, following her. Then he helped her tidy up, but as soon as they'd finished, he strode over to the entertainment unit in the living room. "Come watch a movie with me."

"Um…sure." She followed him more slowly. "Any movie in particular?"

"You choose." He opened the door of a cabinet to reveal racks of DVDs.

Her eyes widened. "That's quite a collection."

"My housekeeper buys a selection for me every couple of months." He took a seat on the black leather sofa.

Her finely arched brows drew together. "I wouldn't have taken you for a man who watched movies."

He shrugged. "I have to unwind sometimes."

For a few seconds she was silent as if weighing his words, though he wasn't sure he liked her deciphering him. She'd probably get some idiotic idea that sometimes he felt a sense of aloneness inside this apartment. That sometimes at the end of the day he would like to share a peaceful moment or two with a woman who understood him. He grimaced inwardly. Of course, Gabrielle understood him a bit too much at times for his liking.

She walked over to the collection and began rifling through the DVDs. "What about this one?" she said, holding up a fairly tame thriller that had been a huge success a couple of years ago.

"As long as it doesn't give you ideas," he joked, and saw her mouth twitch with amusement before she popped the DVD in and went to sit on the chair opposite.

He patted the space beside him. "Sit next to me."

She hesitated. Then, "Is that an order?"

He gave a wry smile. She was a challenge, this one. Every step of the way. "No, a request."

She inclined her head and did as he asked, but still sat a foot away from where he wanted her to be. "Closer," he murmured.

"I'm fine right here."

He leaned over and half lifted her next to him. "Closer," he insisted. "And *that's* an order."

"Damien, I—"

"Shh. The movie's starting."

She remained tense for another ten seconds or so, then he could feel her begin to relax slightly, which was just as well because if she didn't stop arguing he would have to kiss her into submission.

As it was, he would wait to make love to her until after the movie. Oh, he knew he could have her right now, just as he'd done last night on the yacht. Her body was emitting a million little signals that told him she wanted him again.

But like the most delicate tidbit, he would savor her. Call him a masochist, but for five years the memory of this woman had left a burning imprint inside him. Now, to have the very scent of her filling his nostrils, the curve of her bare shoulder beneath his palm, the warmth of her body next to him, was driving him mad again with appreciation and anticipation.

For this woman, he would linger.

Halfway through the movie she kicked off her shoes…and the lingering was over.

"You know," he murmured, his eyes resting on those beautiful toes. "I find your feet very sexy."

Her head snapped away from watching the television. Red rushed into her cheeks. "Um…they're only feet."

"Not to me. Here. Put them up here on my lap. Let me look at them."

A humorous gleam showed in her eyes. "You don't have a foot fetish, do you?"

His mouth tilted in a sardonic grin. "No." Her feet were just a starting point, gorgeous though they were. He would make love to every inch of her.

Starting with those feet.

"Lean back," he said, lifting them onto his lap, forcing her into reclining back against the cushions. He began to slowly trace the pads of his fingers over her delicate toes. "These are very feminine."

She expelled a surprisingly sultry laugh that rippled along his spine. "I would hope so."

He held up one slender foot. "See this arch? It tells me you're a sensual person."

She moistened her lips. "Um…it does?"

"Now if I were to kiss the top of your foot—" he did as he said "—like this."

"Damien…"

Her breathlessness turned him on, not to mention

her dress had crept back along a length of slender thigh. "You don't like that?"

"Yes," she whispered. "I do."

He kissed her ankle. "Too much?"

There was a tiny pause. "Perhaps."

"Not enough?"

All at once she tried to sit up. "The movie. We're supposed to be—"

He grabbed the remote and flicked it off, bathing them in muted light from the dining area across the room. "I'd rather watch *you*," he said, sliding to his knees on the plush carpet and helping her to stretch out before him on the sofa, just like that delectable meal she had prepared for him. "Lie there and enjoy it, Gabrielle."

She licked her lower lip. "What are you going to do?"

"Make love to you with my mouth," he said thickly, watching as her blue eyes caught instant fire. "Would you like that?"

"Er, maybe," she whispered, making him smile at her slight rebellion. Even now, with her body crying out for his touch, she was determined to hold something of herself back.

And he would make sure she gave in.

Totally.

He took possession of those luscious lips, and a few heartbeats later he heard her sigh of sweet surrender that told him she'd only been fighting herself, not him.

And then he explored the smooth, velvet warmth inside her mouth that drew his tongue back time and time again over her moistness, marking her as his own, sending a vibration of arousal through him that made

him suddenly wonder who was the one being pos-
sessed here.

He broke off the kiss and inhaled a deep shuddering
breath. He wanted to consume her, to let his tongue
glide her to a climax, over the hills and valleys of her
body…the peaked nipples, her flat stomach, the slight
rise to her femininity. He only had to lift her in his arms,
and he'd be able to place his lips anywhere he liked.

But first, he did what he promised to do and went
back to her feet and lingered there, touching and strok-
ing. Then he worked his way up one leg, inching up her
dress, placing a kiss on the lacy blue triangle of material
at the apex of her thighs before starting down the other
leg.

Her floral dress had tiny buttons along the front of
it, and he enjoyed undoing them and exposing her
smooth skin by degrees. Until he got to the scar on the
smooth skin of her stomach, and full-blown pain went
right through him. He couldn't stand to think of her
hurt like this, her soft skin having been ripped apart by
the metal of a machine driven by some nitwit who
deserved to be ripped apart himself.

With my bare hands.

"Damien?" she said softly, but there was understanding in her tone.

Her voice pulled him back from the brink and he
made a sound wrenched from deep inside and forced
himself to move on. Otherwise she might think he was
hesitating out of distaste. And he wasn't. Nothing could
be further from the truth.

"It's okay," he said in a brusque voice, then placed

his lips against the scar, hearing her gasp as he kissed the puckered skin.

And then he continued up her silken belly to her round, firm breasts that fit seamlessly in his hands. His heartbeat throbbed in his ears as he took first one swollen caramel nipple into his mouth, then the other, and sucked until she arched her back, raising her desire and in turn thickening the blood in his own veins.

"Damien," she moaned, his name slipping through her lips, her hands gripping his shoulders, her fingers kneading him.

He lifted his head and looked down at Gabrielle's glowing face. She was absolutely beautiful. Absolutely desirable. He knew it was time to taste the rest of her.

Inch by inch he moved back along the way he'd come, retracing his kisses, trailing his lips along to find the exotic scent of her that laced his blood with heat and something so primitive it belonged to just the two of them. Never had he wanted another woman as he wanted Gabrielle. Never would he take from another woman what he knew Gabrielle could give him…had always given him.

Herself.

He stripped the blue panties from her and lowered his mouth, loving the soft cry she gave as he began melting her with strokes of his tongue, eliciting a long moan from her. Small tremors started to ripple through her body, then strengthen. He kept on loving her, could feel her coming, shuddering beneath his mouth, her muscles tensing until she cried out with sheer release. He lapped her up in a flood of pleasure, urging her to even greater heights, to an even greater glory.

She held there.

Held longer than he expected.

He could wait no longer to be inside her. He needed to feel her muscles tightening around him. He needed to make her climax again but this time with him inside her.

He took a condom out of his pocket, ripped off his clothes and joined her on the sofa, entering her with one thrust, groaning into her mouth with the sheer enjoyment of having her slick flesh surround him.

And then a flame licked along his skin and he began to move, felt the tight clenching of her body that intensified with each plunge inside her. She pervaded his senses, clouded his mind and suddenly the world shimmied and he lost the ability to think. His body lost control.

And he lost his mind.

Seven

Gabrielle opened her eyes the next morning and found Damien asleep next to her in bed. He lay on his stomach with his face half turned into the pillow. It made him look so sexy, so rawly masculine.

He murmured something and she stilled. She didn't want to wake him. Not yet. Not when she could study him so freely. Not when she could take pleasure in every detail, noting the way his firm lips were relaxed, seeing the way his chin, too, seemed less arrogant.

Or maybe that was because he needed a shave, she mused as her gaze slowly lowered over the wide shoulders and trim waist, down to where the sheet hugged his hips and flanks, the urge to run her fingers along his spine so very tempting.

He made a sound that for anyone else would be a soft

snore, but not for Damien Trent, and she bit her lip to stop herself from laughing. If only she could tease him about this. But he was not the sort of man you could tease and get away with it.

But did she want to get away with it?

Perhaps not.

At the thought her pleasure faded. A feeling suddenly consolidated in her chest, everything becoming crystal-clear. Damien touched the deepest part of her and it frightened her, causing a wave of panic to riot through her veins. She turned away and buried her face against her pillow, wanting to hide from herself but unable to do so.

Dear God, she had fallen in love with the man who'd stolen her heart five years ago.

She had fallen in love with Damien Trent.

For the second time.

Just then the man she now knew she loved…the man beside her…started to move and wake up. She was tempted to jump up and run from the room, but she'd only be drawing attention to herself. If he came after her and started making love to her again, how would she react now she knew she loved him again? How would she manage to keep everything inside her until she had time to think this all over? Because suddenly the goal-posts had changed. And how that would affect her she wasn't sure.

So she lay there with her back to him and kept her eyes shut, pretending to be asleep, feeling him go up on one elbow and kiss her bare shoulder. She held back a moan, unable to turn toward him and end up in his arms again. She just prayed her didn't draw her over to face him.

And then the mattress dipped slightly as he rolled out of bed, and she expelled a silent sigh of relief. She heard him walk into the bathroom and the shower came on and a few moments later she could hear the sound of water hitting naked flesh. She could almost see the water spraying off his wide shoulders, over his chest, down the arrow of hair. She shut her mind off. She had to or she might just be tempted to join him, and right now she dare not.

Instead of getting up for her own shower, she forced herself to stay in a sort of mental limbo until he'd finished dressing. Then, just when she thought he was about to leave the room and go get some breakfast, his lips touched hers in a brief kiss.

Her lashes flew open in alarm, but all he said was, "Sleep in. Come to the office when you're ready." He started for the door.

It took her a few seconds to register what he'd said. "What?" She sat up. "Where are you going?"

He stopped at the door and turned. "To the office."

"Yours or—"

"Ours?" he joked.

She threw back the covers. "I'm not playing at this, Damien. I don't want to be just a figurehead and leave you to do all the work."

He looked surprised. "I don't think that, but it wouldn't hurt you to have a lie-in."

She got out of bed. "I'm used to getting up early and going to work," she reminded him, in case he'd forgotten she'd been a working woman down in Sydney.

His gaze slid over her short, silky cream nightgown

and his eyes darkened, but he made no move toward her. "Okay, if you're determined, then. I have an important meeting this morning so I have to go to my office first. I'll meet you at Kane's about eleven-thirty."

"Fine," she said, already heading for the shower.

An hour later Gabrielle asked her father's personal assistant, Cheryl, to organize a meeting in the boardroom for eleven-thirty. She and Damien still had things to discuss from yesterday with the managers.

"It doesn't take you long to start throwing your weight around," Keiran sneered as he came into the office just as she was gathering her papers for the meeting.

Gabrielle hid her surprise. This was the first she'd seen Keiran since he'd stormed out yesterday, but he was obviously back to cause trouble and that made her uneasy. Keiran always picked his target. He must have known that Damien wasn't with her.

"Keiran, don't you have work to do? In your *own* office?"

His mouth twisted. "Cheryl tells me you're having another meeting with the middle managers. It isn't going to help the company, you know. They would be more productive just getting on with their jobs."

"Perhaps you should take your own advice," she said coolly.

He sent her a withering glance. "You know, coz, I can't wait to see you fall flat on your face."

"Then you'll be waiting a long time."

"You think so?"

"I know so."

Just then Cheryl buzzed her on the intercom. Giving

Keiran a hard look, Gabrielle pressed the button and listened as the other woman said that Damien was now in the boardroom with the others.

"I'll be right there, Cheryl." Gabrielle stood. "You're welcome to come to the meeting," she told him as she came around the desk and walked toward the open doorway.

"How generous of you."

She'd had just about enough of him. Her mouth tightened as she went to step past him, but suddenly she somehow missed her step because she felt herself trip on the carpet then fall forward, giving a little squeal. Thankfully the door frame stopped her fall but it still shook her.

It was a couple of seconds before Keiran spoke, and then only after Cheryl came rushing over. "Are you okay?" the PA asked with concern.

"She tripped on the carpet," Keiran was quick to say, but Gabrielle was sure his voice held fake concern.

"I'm fine," Gabrielle said, looking down at the plush carpet, but there were no rips or snags. Then she darted a look at Keiran. For some reason he had enjoyed her being hurt. And that was typical Keiran. He was the type to pull the wings off butterflies.

Keiran's smile was sickly. "You always were one to trip over nothing," he said, but that just wasn't true. She'd never been especially clumsy, so she wasn't sure why he was using that excuse now.

Unless…

She frowned. He wouldn't have tried to hurt her, would he? He was certainly capable of it but could he really be that nasty?

No. She'd tripped by herself that's all. It was just one of those things.

"As long as you're okay." Cheryl said with a frown.

Gabrielle tried to smile warmly. "Thanks for your concern, Cheryl. I'm fine."

The other woman nodded as Keiran bent and picked up the papers Gabrielle had dropped. "Here we go," he said, handing them back to her. "We'll be late for the meeting if we don't hurry."

Gabrielle's brow rose in surprise as she took them. "You're coming?"

He smiled tightly. "Wild horses couldn't keep me away."

Gabrielle turned to head out the door. She'd been very much afraid that was the case.

Later that afternoon the phone rang in the office. Gabrielle had just spent the past hour with Damien poring over some of the paperwork Keiran had worked on, and she was now glad to put it aside for a while. Working so close to Damien was playing havoc on her senses. He smelled gorgeous, and he looked gorgeous, and she kept remembering how he'd seduced her on the sofa last night.

Thankfully they'd had a couple of other interruptions, so at least she was getting Damien in small doses, she mused as she picked up the phone. Damien in large doses was definitely an overdose.

It was her mother, telling her that Keiran had dropped by to see Russell but that she hadn't let him into the room. "Darling, we don't want him to let it slip about your marriage before I've had a chance to tell your father, so I told him to come back tomorrow," Caroline said, making Gabrielle want to kiss her. "But the doctor's just said I can tell Russell when he wakes up, and I know your father will want to see you and Damien once I tell him."

"Should we come to the hospital now, then?" Gabrielle said, seeing Damien's gaze sharpen.

"Yes, Russell's due to wake soon."

Gabrielle said goodbye, then hung up the phone and told Damien what had happened. She scowled. "Do you think Keiran's going to cause trouble?"

Damien's jaw clenched. "What else?"

She thought of something. "I'm surprised he didn't try and tell my mother we'd only married for the sake of the company."

"How do you know he didn't?"

"I'm sure if he'd said something she'd be upset. No, he's kept quiet about it, and that worries me. He's up to something," she muttered.

"It doesn't matter. He can't do anything about it anyway," he said with confidence. "Come on. Let's go. I want to make sure Russell is okay about everything."

Gabrielle hesitated briefly, and only because she was trying to come to terms with something. Damien was genuinely concerned for her parents, and it had nothing to do with money. How hadn't she seen such kindness in him before? Why was she only seeing it now when she was in love with him?

A warm glow stayed with her until she walked into the room at the hospital, and even then her father's joy did her heart good. Russell was actually sitting against the pillows, still weak but growing stronger.

After she kissed him on the cheek, he wagged a finger at Damien beside her, his face smiling like he'd won the lottery. "I always knew you had a thing for my daughter," he said, making Gabrielle start.

Damien grinned ruefully. "I didn't think I'd fooled you back then, Russell. Of course, as soon as I saw her again I knew I couldn't let her get away another time." He kissed her tenderly on the mouth. "Isn't that right, sweetheart?"

For a moment Gabrielle stood looking up at him, trying to find her voice. Oh, how she wished this moment were true.

Her mother made a soft sound from the other side of the bed. "Look at the two of them, Russell. Anyone can see they're in love."

Gabrielle drew her gaze away from Damien, realizing she must look like a lovesick fool. It hadn't been intentional.

"Yes, Caroline, you're right," her father agreed, but Gabrielle noticed he was looking at her mother with an odd longing in his eyes, only her mother didn't appear to notice because she was smiling at Damien. Quickly Gabrielle glanced up at Damien and knew he hadn't missed that look in her father's eyes, either.

Her father reached out for Gabrielle's hand, his eyes filling with deep regret. "Gabrielle, we never meant to hurt you," he said gruffly.

Perhaps loving Damien made her soft…or wiser… but suddenly she realized she was more than ready to forgive this man. "I know that now, Dad." Feeling emotive, she leaned forward and buried her face in his neck, choked up by what this meant. She hated that her father almost had to die before they could all come to their senses. Hated it, yet was oh so grateful for it.

All at once she heard her mother say, "We love you, honey. We're so sorry about what happened."

Gabrielle blinked rapidly to hold back silly tears filled with joy. She loved these two people. She wouldn't cut these ties. She wouldn't even try. Not ever again.

"It's okay. Really," she said, pulling back and putting her hand in her father's. And when her mother reached across the bed, Gabrielle put her hand in her mother's too. They stayed like that for a moment.

Suddenly the door opened and in walked one of the nurses. "What's this?" she teased. "A prayer meeting?"

Gabrielle looked at her parents and smiled as they let go of each other, but she noticed the soft look her father surreptitiously gave her mother. "Sort of," she muttered.

"Nothing wrong with that," the nurse said, walking over to the bed and checking her father's chart as Damien put his arm around Gabrielle's shoulder and pulled her close to him. She leaned into him for once, feeling weak with the emotion of the moment.

The nurse didn't stay long and when the door closed behind her, Caroline smiled at Gabrielle. "I'll have to take you to see your old room, darling. We've left everything as it was."

"I've already seen it, Mum." She stepped forward and kissed her mother's cheek. "Thank you," she murmured, then kissed her father's cheek, too.

Caroline looked as pleased as Russell. "Well, now

you're a married woman with a home of your own," her mother said. "You might want to come and take some of your old things as keepsakes."

Gabrielle arched a brow. "You don't mind?"

"Darling, they're *your* things." Caroline smiled briefly at her husband. "Besides, we already have our daughter. We don't need things to remind us of you."

"Oh, Mum," Gabrielle said, touched beyond measure as she blinked back tears, which then started her mother getting teary-eyed and had her father sniffing slightly, making Damien give a quiet chuckle.

Half an hour later Gabrielle walked into the apartment and dropped her handbag on the sofa. She went to turn toward the kitchen to get a drink of water, but Damien had entered the apartment and was standing behind her. His hands slid around her hips and pulled her up against him.

"What are you doing?" she said, feeling his instant arousal against her. She gave a delicious shudder.

"Reaping the benefits of marriage," he murmured, turning her around to face him. His eyes had a strange seriousness in them that captured her attention.

She moistened her lips. "We didn't have to get married for that."

"I know, but we may as well enjoy it." He started running his lips along her chin.

"But dinner—"

"Can wait," he said, and closed over her mouth with a kiss. A long drugging kiss that sparked an ache inside her and soon had her aflame for him, making everything so much more poignant for her now she knew she loved him. Poignant and incredibly beautiful.

They made love.

Afterward Damien held Gabrielle in his arms. Their lovemaking had been richly satisfying, but he couldn't seem to shake a slight melancholy that seemed to be sitting inside his chest. He didn't lack for anything in his life, yet somehow it felt as though he did. He had the most beautiful woman in the world in his arms, yet absurdly he wanted more from her. Hell, what was the matter with him?

Just then Gabrielle arched her neck to gaze up at him from the crook of his arm. "Did you see the look my father gave my mother? I'm sure he still loves her."

Her words surprised him. Usually she didn't talk after making love. She either fell asleep in his arms, or they both got up and did other things. Their relationship was not usually about sharing the moment after they'd sated their bodies on each other.

"I'm sure he does, too," he agreed, remembering the way Russell had looked at Caroline. "In any case, your mother's already told us she loves your father. It's just a matter of time before they get back together."

Gabrielle sighed. "They've wasted such a lot of years."

So did we, came the unbidden thought. It all fell into place then. The reason he felt unsettled was because of what had happened in the hospital room this afternoon. It must have subconsciously stirred up memories of five years ago.

"Why did you leave, Gabrielle?"

She looked startled. "Um, when?" she asked, lowering her gaze to his chest.

"You know when."

She shrugged, but still kept her eyes downward. "It wasn't easy living with my father after my mother left. And before that it had never been much good, either."

He paused. "No, why did you leave *me?*"

Her eyes lifted and he could see she'd known what he'd meant all along. "I explained it in the note."

And he'd brushed that aside at the time, allowing work commitments to prevail. Nothing and no one had been going to stop him from making his millions. Not even this beautiful woman in his arms.

"Ahh, the note," he murmured, half to himself. "You didn't want me coming after you, if I remember rightly."

She looked uneasy. "That's right."

And that made him wonder. "Why?"

She blinked, then gave a bland smile. "This is beginning to sound like an inquisition," she joked, but her strained look told him she didn't actually find it amusing.

He scowled. "What are you hiding, Gabrielle?"

Something flickered in her eyes, before she glanced downward at their naked bodies entwined on the bed. "Nothing, apparently," she mused.

She wasn't fooling him. She was using sex to get him to change the subject. And that meant she was definitely hiding something.

Or someone.

God, he felt like someone had punched him in the stomach. That thought had never occurred to him before. He'd always assumed *he* was enough for her.

He squared his shoulders, prepared for a blow. "Was there another man involved?"

Her eyes widened in total surprise. "What! No, of course not."

Fierce relief washed over him. He began to breathe again. "Just as well," he growled. "You're my wife now and if another man comes looking for you, I'll kill him."

She stared for a moment, clearly surprised. Then her eyes softened. "Damien, you have no need to worry. I won't be leaving you again."

He expelled a breath. For once she didn't sound as if their marriage was a fate worse than death, and suddenly he felt more than pleased about that. He'd never realized before how much he'd missed by *not* being married. He was enjoying being able to work alongside Gabrielle, coming home with her, sharing dinner, sleeping together. They were a couple.

And one day they might even have a family.

He swallowed hard. The thought of Gabrielle carrying his child made him feel kind of strange. Like he was standing on shifting sand.

"Damien?" she said in a low voice, querying his silence, sending him into action.

He eased her off him and rolled out of bed. "Let's get something to eat," he muttered, standing, glad to be back on solid ground.

The sound of water running in the shower roused Gabrielle at four the next morning. For a moment she lay there half-awake, remembering the feel of Damien's lips on hers after they'd gone to bed. He'd taken her with his body, conquering her, dividing her, seeming to know what she wanted before she did. It had made for an incredible union.

She must have fallen asleep again because she woke to the sound of water still running in the shower. This time her eyelids flew open. What on earth was Damien *doing* in there?

She threw back the covers and hurried into the bathroom. And stopped dead when she saw him naked in the shower, his forehead pressed against the tiled wall as if he didn't have the energy to hold himself up.

"Oh my God," she said, racing across the room. She slid the glass door back, thankful to find the water cold. "Damien? Are you all right? What's the matter?"

He looked up at her groggily. "I was hot," he mumbled, his eyes not really focusing on her, his cheeks flushed.

She felt his forehead. His skin was warm despite the cold water running over him. "You've got a fever," she said, turning the taps off.

He seemed to become aware of her. "Allergy."

A slice of panic raced through her. Allergies could be life threatening. "You need an ambulance."

"No!" He tried to straighten up. "My doctor. He knows. Call him."

Her panic receded as common sense took hold. If it had been life threatening, Damien would be dead by now. Oh God, she couldn't think that.

She took him by the arm. "Let me help you back to bed."

He made a feeble attempt to step out of the cubicle. "I can make it," he said, then swayed as he tried to stand by himself.

"I'm sure," she said wryly, grabbing a towel to throw over his shoulders and dry him, but he pulled it away and wrapped it around his trim hips, looking thoroughly sexy and masculine. "Here. Lean on me."

"I'm too heavy."

"Just lean a little, then. I can manage." She slowly led him back to the bedroom and helped him down on the bed. He groaned when his head touched the pillow, and she frowned as she looked down at him. "I'll go call your doctor."

"Good," he rasped.

She hurried away and made the call after finding his doctor's private number in the address book by the telephone. Thankfully the doctor seemed to take it in his stride that he was being called out before dawn.

When she came back, Damien had fallen asleep. His cheeks were flushed and he started mumbling. It was obvious he was a little delirious and that worried her. The doctor said he knew the problem and would come straight around, so she hoped he kept to his word. She didn't like seeing Damien like this.

All at once he started to move restlessly. "Mum?"

Oh, heavens. "Damien?"

"I'm sorry, Mum. Sorry I couldn't be…" He trailed off to sleep again, making Gabrielle wondered what he'd been about to say.

Just then the doctor arrived. "It's a food allergy," the older man said after she let him into the apartment and they went into the bedroom. "Some sort of preservative. It makes him dizzy and gives him a fever. He must have eaten some of it last night." He put his bag down on the bed and gave Damien a cursory glance. "Do you know what he had for dinner?"

"Our housekeeper cooked lasagna, but I'm sure she must know about the allergy." Gabrielle couldn't imagine Damien risking this too often.

The doctor opened his bag and started to prepare an injection. "It's hard to tell what's in some foods. He might've got a good dose of it by accident."

Deep concern filled her. "Isn't there anything you can do about it?"

"There's some allergy tests, but he won't have them done. He says he can handle it." His eyes held a rueful glint.

She found herself smiling back at him, relieved more than anything that he was here. "That sounds like Damien."

He gave the injection, then looked up at her again. "By the way, I'm Ken. I've been Damien's doctor for a few years now. I believe you're the new Mrs. Trent."

Her cheeks warmed. "So word's out?"

"Definitely. And there are a few very disappointed ladies around the place, let me tell you."

She pushed aside a sense of jealousy and let her mouth quirk with humor. "I'm sure they'll get over it." Not like her. She loved him too much to lose him again.

He gave her a speculative look, then nodded in approval. "You'll be good for him."

"I know," she said, serious now.

Ken left not long after, saying he'd be back before lunch to check on his patient. Reassured that Damien was okay, she made herself a cup of coffee then curled up on the luxurious leather club chair by the window and watched him as he slept. It was a rare opportunity to look at the man she loved, without fear of him catching her.

At that thought she blinked. Good Lord. This is what it had come down to. Her sneaking peeks at Damien to satisfy the longing in her heart. Yet she couldn't seem to stop herself. Everything about him… every feeling for him…was a precious thing to be cherished and savored.

It was just the way it was.

A few hours later he woke her, trying to get out of bed. "Damien?"

Sitting on the edge of the mattress, he turned his head slowly, his gaze sliding across the room at her. "What are you doing over there?"

"I fell asleep in the chair," she said, getting to her feet.

He paused while he swallowed. "You should have gone to the spare room."

"You might have needed me."

Another pause. "I'm fine," he said, but he didn't move.

She walked over to him. "Where are you going, anyway?"

"To the bathroom…then the office."

She raised an eyebrow. "Really? You can't even stand up. Besides, it's Saturday. There's no need to go anywhere."

"I work every day." But he still sat there, like he was trying to get his balance. "Is Ken coming back?"

"Later this morning." She touched his forehead and frowned at his damp skin. "Perhaps you should see about getting something done about this allergy?"

His mouth set. "No."

She let that go. "Come on. I'll take you to the bathroom."

"I can do it myself." He pushed himself up, then rocked on his feet.

"You're one stubborn man," she declared, pulling his arm around her shoulder. "Come on."

A few minutes later she had him back in bed. "You were delirious earlier on, you know," she said, trying to get through his thick skull this was serious and she had been very worried about him.

"I don't remember," he said, closing his eyes.

"You were talking to your mother."

His eyelids shot open, and a hint of the old Damien was back. "Is that so?"

"You were talking about being sorry." She considered him. "You really shouldn't keep things inside you, Damien. It's not good for you."

"Perhaps I'll hire a publicist," he mocked, but it was weak at best.

She hid a smile. "I can see you're starting to get better."

"Yes. So stop mothering me."

She winced inwardly even as she angled her chin. "I'm so glad my services are appreciated." She turned on her heels and headed for the door. Of all the ungrateful…

"Gabrielle?"

Hurt, she wanted to tell him to drop dead, but the memories of finding him in the shower were still fresh in her mind. She stopped at the door and turned to look at him. "Yes?"

"I'm sorry." His eyes softened with gratitude. "Thank you for looking after me."

Oh, she was such a weak woman where he was concerned, she decided, as tender warmth entered her heart. "You're welcome."

Eight

After that, life went into a holding pattern for a few days. Kia and Danielle took turns phoning, breezily chatting about Gabrielle's new Porsche that they'd heard Damien had bought for her, but really to see how she was coping with married life. Gabrielle tried to sound upbeat and positive. She thought she did a pretty good job of convincing them she was okay, but there was still a hint of worry in their voices that made her realize she wasn't really fooling them at all.

Somehow they knew she loved Damien.

Really loved him.

But they never mentioned it to her. She was pretty sure they didn't mention it to their husbands, either, for which she was eternally grateful.

As for Damien, he gave nothing away, but every

night he made love to her with a passion that made her love for him deepen. Beyond that she was afraid to think. She couldn't let herself. There was just too much of a heartache standing between them. A heartache he had no idea existed. One she prayed he *never* knew existed, not just for her sake but for his own. The more she loved him, the more she didn't want to see him hurt.

And then one evening after dinner, Damien had gone downstairs to get some paperwork he'd left in his BMW when his cell phone rang. Gabrielle wasn't sure whether to answer it at first, but thoughts of her father taking a turn for the worse had her hurrying over to the coffee table to snatch it up.

A woman gave a little gasp, then hesitated. "Er…is Damien there?" the husky voice said on the other end of the phone.

Gabrielle's heart sank as she wondered if this was one of the women Ken had said was "disappointed" about Damien's marriage. "He's stepped out for a moment."

"Oh."

She did sound disappointed, but Gabrielle wasn't sure it was because she knew he had a wife now. "He'll be back soon."

There was a tiny pause. "To whom am I speaking?" the woman asked, but not in a nasty way. She actually sounded rather well-bred and polite.

"Gabrielle." She almost said "his wife," but just didn't have the heart. "Can I tell him who called?"

"Um, yes. Please tell him Cynthia called. Perhaps he could call me back? It's important."

"I'll pass the message on," Gabrielle said as an unexpected feeling of jealousy hit her. Cynthia sounded like a nice person, and that was more dangerous than a hundred women who only wanted Damien for what they could get from him.

Just as she hung up, Damien walked into the apartment, looking so handsome he made her heart skip a beat.

"Who was that?" he said, lightly tossing his car keys on the table.

"Someone called Cynthia."

He looked at her sharply. "Did she say what she wanted?"

"You."

His eyes narrowed, telling her he got her point. "Does she want me to call her back?"

"Yes." She paused. "An old girlfriend?"

A shadow of annoyance crossed his face. "She's a…woman friend."

"Your mistress?" His words stabbed at her heart. She'd suspected, but hearing him say it out loud made her feel sick. "I expect you to be faithful, Damien."

His gaze held hers. "Who said I wouldn't be?"

"Then you'd better let all your…*women* friends know you're married now."

He held himself stiffly. "I'll be faithful, Gabrielle. You have no need to worry on that score."

Yes, but would he feel the same way in a few years' time? Men often played around, and rich successful men were no different. Most of them thought it was their right. Her father certainly had.

He walked over to her, captured her chin with his fingertips and tilted her face up to him. "Listen to me, Gabrielle. And I mean this." His eyes turned even more intense than usual. "You're all the woman I want."

"Am I?" she croaked, unable to stop the sinking feeling in her stomach at his words.

Want, he'd said.

Not *need*.

"Yes."

"Lucky me," she managed to say.

He stared at her, baffled. Then, "Perhaps I should show you just how lucky you are," he said, arrogance taking over as he scooped her up in his arms and strode toward the bedroom.

By the time she came up for air, he'd made love to her as if he'd wanted to imprint himself on her forever. And yes, she felt very lucky indeed. For a moment she reveled in that feeling. But then she realized he was only stamping what he considered to be *his*.

Yet despite fighting her feelings for a man who would try to control her if he knew she loved him, Gabrielle was happy to work alongside Damien at the office, helping him make changes that would benefit the company. She was impressed, not only by his business acumen, but by his consideration in teaching her things about the business that would take her a lifetime to learn elsewhere. Yet they both knew who was really in charge.

Him.

Not that she minded. She needed him to put the company back on the right track. Perhaps if Keiran hadn't messed things up so badly she might have stood half a chance of straightening things out herself. As it was, she was grateful for Damien's help.

And everyone was grateful that Keiran had taken a break from work the past few days. The office was a much nicer place without him around, putting her on edge, constantly sending her daggers with his eyes. She could easily see why all the department heads had been leaving for greener pastures. Thankfully the ones who hadn't left were now happy to stay, and Damien had even managed to get two of their top staff to return to their old positions.

Unfortunately, Keiran came back to work the morning Damien was absent at an important meeting. It didn't take her cousin long to walk into her office with a smug look on his face that somehow sent shivers down her spine and gave her a sense of déjà vu. She hoped she was wrong but she had the feeling he was up to something.

She gave him a cool look. "Do you think you could make an appointment with Cheryl? I'm a busy lady these days."

He came toward her. "Cheryl isn't at her desk."

"Then perhaps you could wait until she is."

He flopped down on the chair opposite her. "But I wanted to tell you something really important. I'm sure you'll find it fascinating."

She looked into his gloating eyes and knew he had trouble in mind.

"Guess where I've been?" he taunted, as was his way.

She picked up her pen, ready to ignore him. "Keiran, I don't have time for—"

"Sydney," he cut across her.

A wave of apprehension replaced that shiver down her spine. "What's so important about that?"

His mouth spread in a thin-lipped smile. "Ahh, but it's not what I did in Sydney. It's what I found out."

The breath seemed to have solidified in her throat. "Found out?"

"About you."

She blinked, hoping she sounded suitably surprised, but inside she was shaking. "Me?"

"Yes. And it was something very, very interesting."

Dear Lord, could Keiran know?

"Really?" she said, leaning back in her chair. She wouldn't…couldn't…let him see how fast her heart was thumping in her chest.

"I took one of your friends out to dinner."

Oh God.

She arched a brow. "One of *my* friends?"

"Simone."

As casually as she could, she managed to shrug. "Simone isn't really a friend of mine. I worked with her, that's all."

"Well, give the woman a bit of attention and she was happy to tell me *all* about you."

All?

Ignoring him, Gabrielle sat straighter in her chair and looked down at her paperwork, poised to write. Anything but let him see how afraid she was. "There's nothing to tell."

"Come on, Gabrielle," he scoffed. "You sit there looking all innocent, but underneath you have a dirty little secret."

Her head snapped up. "I don't know what you mean."

"You were in a car accident."

He knew.

Dear God, he knew.

"Tell me something I don't know," she scoffed back.

"You were pregnant." He paused for effect. "You lost the baby."

She swallowed hard. "I still don't know what you're talking about, Keiran," she said, but her voice wobbled and gave her away.

Keiran's eyes lit with a sick sort of triumph. "I wonder if that new husband of yours would be interested in all this? He thinks he's got a saint for a wife."

She squared her shoulders. "I never claimed to be a saint, Keiran."

"So you don't think he'd be interested in knowing you had an affair and carried another man's child?"

Her head reeled back. So he didn't know it was Damien's child. She wasn't sure right now if that was a good or a bad thing. And what did it matter, anyway? He was determined to destroy her.

"I see *that* got your attention," he drawled.

Needing to do something, she got to her feet and walked over to the window. "What do you want?" she said, keeping her back to him, looking out through the glass but seeing nothing.

"So you're admitting you were pregnant?"

She stiffened but didn't turn around. "I can't very well deny it, can I?"

"No, you can't."

All at once she'd had enough. This was her *cousin* doing this to her, for heaven's sake. How dare he threaten her in this way!

She spun around and glared at him. "Blackmail really is an ugly word, Keiran. It suits you."

"Sticks and stones," he mocked. Then his face turned deadly serious. "I tell you what I want. I'll give you one week. One week until your father gets home and is on the mend properly, then I want you to pack up and leave. For good this time."

She felt the blood drain from her face. "Wh-what?"

"You'll tell Damien you made a mistake, and you'll tell your folks you really couldn't put their past behind you. And you'll sign over twenty percent of your shares to me and tell everyone you think I'm the best man for the job. Then you get the hell out of our lives for good. I intend to take over again and I will. By the time Russell is better, this company will be well and truly under my control."

Despair cut the air from her lungs. "You're crazy."

"Yes, but I'll be *rich* and crazy."

"You have money now."

"Not like dear ol' Uncle Russell," he derided. "See, I want it all. Every single cent. Every bit of power." He puffed up his chest. "People will respect me from now on."

She realized that was the one thing no one had ever given him. *Respect.* But then, respect had to be earned. And this man didn't ever have a chance of that happening.

She tried to remain calm. Call his bluff. "I wonder what your parents will say if I tell them what you're doing?"

His eyes flared with anger. "Don't even try it, Gabrielle," he warned through gritted teeth.

"Why not? I could go see them and tell them everything. I'm sure they'd be very interested." Her father's brother, Evan, and his wife, Karen, had always supported their son in all his endeavors, yet Gabrielle had sensed a deep disappointment in them. She didn't think what she had to say would surprise them at all.

Keiran's anger disappeared, replaced by a coldness that chilled her to the bone. "Oh, but then I'd have to tell yours all about you and your sordid past, wouldn't I? How do you think your father will take the news that his precious daughter isn't as precious as he thinks? Do you think it'll upset him? Perhaps even bring on another stroke?" His lips twisted at her gasp. "You have a lot more to lose than I do, *coz.*"

She expelled a defeated breath. He was right. No matter what, Keiran would bounce back even if it meant sacrificing his relationship with his parents.

She and her parents, on the other hand…

"Please leave," she said, walking to the door and opening it.

Insolently he stood up and walked toward her. "One week, Gabrielle," he whispered when he reached her. Then he saw Cheryl at her desk in the other office, and he smiled at Gabrielle as he picked up her hand and kissed the back of it. "And then it's bye-bye," he murmured.

Gabrielle winced with pain, not just in her heart but physical pain. He was squeezing the inside of her wrist with his other hand, hurting her. She tried to tug away but he held on a moment more, digging his fingers in while looking at her with eyes that blazed a shocking hatred.

"Don't forget what's at stake here," he reminded her.

She angled her chin at him, determined not to let him see her cower. "I won't forget," she said pointedly. She'd never forget, nor forgive him, for this.

His smirk acknowledged her comment, and finally he dropped her hand and said nothing more. She had to stop herself from rubbing her tenderized skin. She wouldn't give him that satisfaction.

Then he strode toward his own office, throwing Cheryl a satisfied smile on the way. For the life of her, Gabrielle couldn't manage a smile for her PA. Instead she shut the door and sank back against it, her legs barely holding her up. A tear rolled down her cheek as raw grief threatened to overwhelm her.

Oh God, how could she keep the secret of her miscarriage from the man she loved? Even if she threw caution to the wind and told Damien about their child... and she'd sworn never to do that...she still couldn't stay now. Once he discovered her deception, he would never forgive her.

Yet how could she *not* tell him something so important? What if years from now he found out about the baby and how the accident had caused her to lose their child? Their marriage would have been based on even more deception all that time.

A deceptive lie.

As it was now.

But there wasn't only Damien to think about. For her father's sake, she couldn't tell Damien the truth and risk him destroying everything her father had worked so hard to achieve. And he *would* destroy Russell Kane if he knew her father had told her to leave all those years ago, despite her father not knowing she was pregnant. She had no doubt about that.

Neither could she risk Keiran getting to her father

and doing his worst. And she couldn't tell her father herself. Keiran was right. The shock of her accident, let alone her losing her unborn baby, could bring on another stroke. And this time he may not recover.

Of course, when she left in a week's time it could very well bring on another stroke then, too. But what was worse? Telling her parents she wanted to go back to Sydney, letting them think she was unhappy here in Darwin but allowing herself to keep in touch with them? Or telling them about the loss of their unborn grandchild…and the anguish she had gone through alone five years ago…both sure to cause them grief.

No, somehow she had to find the strength to walk away from her parents a second time.

And from Damien.

From love entirely.

Nine

Gabrielle wasn't sure whether to be thankful or not when Damien left a message to say he'd be tied up for the rest of the day. At least she wouldn't have to put on an act for him, though how she was going to hide a breaking heart she wasn't sure. But somehow she would do it. She had to. This last week with him would be so very special. The memory of it had to last her for the rest of her life.

Just as she walked in the apartment after work, her mother phoned to say they'd sent her father home from hospital earlier in the afternoon. Wanting to share the good news, and wondering when Damien would be home for dinner, Gabrielle phoned him on his cell phone, expecting to leave a message. And was surprised when he answered.

"Are you going to see him?" he asked, after she'd finished telling him the news.

"I thought I might go over after dinner once he's had a chance to rest."

"If you can wait half an hour, I'll be able to come with you."

She blinked. "Um…okay."

An infinitesimal pause came down the line. "Better yet. Let's grab a pizza, go down to the beach and eat it, then we'll drop by the house and see Russell."

Her stomach did a flip-flop.

"Gabrielle?"

"Yes?"

"Is there a problem with that?"

Her problem was in loving him.

And having to leave him.

"No. That would be lovely," she said huskily.

"Fine. See you soon."

Gabrielle hung up the phone with a moan of inner pain. Before Keiran's ultimatum today she would have been secretly thrilled to share a pizza with Damien on a tropical beach. Perhaps she could have even let her guard down enough to enjoy herself. But now her heart was turning over as though it wanted to lie down and die.

Not that she let Damien see her thoughts when he arrived home just as she was walking out of the bedroom after showering and changing into something more casual. He looked so gorgeous that her heart started to pitter-patter like the sound of a rain shower.

Putting his briefcase down beside the sofa, he discarded his jacket before turning to look at her, his gaze sliding over her cream linen shorts and white tank top. "You look really nice."

The breath stalled in her throat at that look. "Thank you."

He started walking toward her, his eyes never leaving her face as he loosened his tie. "I'm hungry."

All at once she felt strangely excited. "Then we'd better—"

He gently captured her by the arm, his gaze burning a fire for her. "For you, Gabrielle."

Anticipation sent a feeling of exhilaration through her. "Oh."

His other hand slipped around her neck and pulled her closer. "I'm been thinking about doing this all day," he drawled huskily, looking down at her open lips as if he wanted to kiss them right off her.

She moistened them anyway. "Really?"

He hovered just above her mouth. "Why are you surprised?"

His warm breath wafted over her. "Er, we only made love this morning."

A muscle ticked in his cheek. "I could have you ten times a day and still want more."

She suddenly felt boneless.

"Go on, Gabrielle. Say it."

Her heart pounded. "What?"

"That you feel the same." He ran a fingertip over her lower lip. "Be honest."

Of all the things that she *couldn't* be honest about with this man, this wasn't one of them. And what would it hurt to tell him the truth this once? This time next week she'd be remembering this moment and wishing she was back here in his arms.

"Yes," she admitted into the hushed stillness. "I feel the same."

Satisfaction crossed his face as he placed her hands on his chest, her palms against his shirt, letting her feel his body warmth. "Then make love to me."

Her heart skipped a beat. "You mean—"

"Take the initiative this time. Take the clothes off me. Then take me inside you," he said, his voice growing hoarse. "That's where I need to be right now."

For the space of a heartbeat they stared at each other. "Damien, I—" She wasn't even sure what she was going to say. She was just playing for time. She wanted him inside her, too, but was very much afraid that if she touched him like he wanted, she'd give herself away.

His green eyes glinted. "Do it, Gabrielle. You know you want to."

Yes, she did. Very much, but since her return she'd never really been game enough. Always it had been Damien making the first move. Damien who drew her close in bed, held her tight. Damien who caught her to him when she walked by him and pulled her on his lap.

Yet she did want to make love to him. And suddenly his very need for her gave her the courage to be bold. She would show him what she couldn't say.

"Yes, I want to," she said softly. She wouldn't think about tomorrow. This moment is what mattered.

He expelled a breath. "Go for it," he muttered hoarsely.

She paused only briefly before looking down at his half undone tie. He looked so casually sexy, so half-undone himself, that the breath hitched in her throat. She didn't want to spoil this picture of him. She could stand here and stare at him for hours.

But she needed to move on, so with shaky hands she began to finish the job of undoing the tie for him. She tossed the silky material on the plush carpet, then continued, slowly undoing the buttons on his shirt, one by one, feeling his heartbeat thudding beneath her hands, his personal male scent embracing her senses.

She gave a soft little sigh as her palms slipped inside his open shirt and skimmed over the wall of his powerful chest. She loved the feel of hard muscle softened by taut skin.

"You're gorgeous," she murmured, saying what she thought, seeing surprised pleasure flicker in his eyes. It made love rise up inside her, urged her on. She leaned forward and traced the tip of her tongue in the light mat of hair on his chest. "Mmm, you taste salty."

He released a guttural sound that reminded her of the feminine power she'd wielded years ago. Back then she'd had no such inhibitions once Damien had initiated her into the ways of making love. Now it was all coming back.

She inhaled him in. "In fact, you smell like a man who's ready for some loving."

A pulse leaped along his throat. "Then love me," he rasped, making her heart turn over, knowing he only meant physical love but willing to give him more.

She didn't need any further encouragement. She pushed his shirt the rest of the way off and dropped it on the floor. Then she let herself wander, teasing him with her hands and with her lips over the smooth golden skin, circling his nipple with the tip of her tongue, hearing another groan rise up from inside him before she transferred to the other side of his chest.

And then she trailed feather-soft kisses down through the dark hair in the center of his chest, arrowing down further to his belt buckle at his trim waist. She could see the effect she had on him even before she straightened and undid the buckle, lowering the zipper on his trousers, freeing him from his underpants.

He was gloriously aroused. All male and rigid muscle encased in warm satin. She slipped her hand around him and caressed him, loving the sound of the ragged groan he gave.

"Witch."

"You want me to stop?" she said, arching a provocative eyebrow.

"What do you think?" he growled.

She smiled. "What I *think* is that I'm going to have my way with you."

"Yes."

She looked down to where her hand held him. And her head lowered. And then for long minutes she made love to him with her hands and her mouth, tasting him with her lips and tongue, breathing him in, *loving* him, until he put her from him with a sharp hiss as he pulled her upward.

He caught her face between his hands and gave her a brief hard kiss. "I need you naked against me."

Her pulse was already racing through her veins, and his words sent it skyrocketing. "Then let me do the honors," she whispered, stepping back and undressing for him, quick not slow, wanting him now, too much tension between them.

She gasped in delight when he pulled her to him and his erection pressed up against her, hard and demanding. She savored the feel of his hot skin next to hers, the touch of his hands sliding up and down her bare back, the way the hair of his chest brushed against her aching nipples.

And then he swung her up in his arms and headed into the bedroom, tumbling her down on the comforter. "I thought I was supposed to be in charge here," she reminded him huskily.

He ignored that as he quickly protected himself with a condom before joining her on the bed.

Then he lifted her on top of him. "There." Adjusting them both, he eased her down on his thick shaft. "Take charge," he muttered as she took him into her.

An hour and a half later they were sitting on a blanket under the coconut palms on Mindil Beach, eating pizza and watching the glorious sunset. She was famished after another round of lovemaking in the shower before they'd dressed again and left the apartment.

But she still felt as if she was on sensation overload by just having him next to her, watching her with a speculative look in his eyes that belied his casual appearance.

"So, how did it go at the office today?" he said in a conversational tone, just like they were the usual married couple.

She winced inwardly. The usual married couple were in love. Neither did the usual married couple have a cousin blackmailing the wife, threatening to destroy every thing she held dear.

"Um…it was a challenge.".

He nodded, and there was a pause as he took a bite of the pizza and looked out to sea. He would have no idea just how much of a "challenge" Keiran had been today.

All at once he turned his head to look at her, studying her thoughtfully for a moment. Then, "I want you to go back to university and finish your degree."

She almost dropped her food. "What!"

Amusement briefly twinkled in his eyes, before he grew serious again. "When I first met you, you were at university studying for your Bachelor of Nutrition and Dietetics. Your eyes used to light up whenever you talked about it, so I'm assuming you regret not finishing it. Am I right?"

"I guess so but—"

"Finish it, Gabrielle."

She dropped her gaze to the pizza in her hand. "I…I can't."

"Why not?"

How could she tell him that soon she had to go back to making a living? Eileen would have her back, but there wouldn't be time leftover for study.

She shrugged. "It's not something I ever think about."

"Then promise me you *will* think about it."

She looked over at him. "I promise," she said truthfully. She'd already thought about it, but that's all she could do.

"Good."

She tilted her head and watched the soft breeze ruffle his dark hair. Suddenly she was greedy. She wanted to know everything she could about this man before she set him free.

"What are *your* dreams, Damien? You never told me."

He took a sip from his can of cola and swallowed the liquid, then his lips curved in a wry smile. "What every man wants. To be rich, successful and have any woman he desires."

She grimaced. It was typical of him not to share his dreams with her, yet he expected her to tell him everything. "I'm serious."

His smile disappeared. "Seriously, then. I'm rich. I'm successful. And I've got the woman I desire."

Her heart turned all aquiver. "Oh."

His eyes assessed hers. "Is that all you've got to say?"

"Three out of three ain't bad," she joked, but felt far from laughing. A man like Damien would never truly admit to actually feeling something for a woman, other than lust. And that was just as well. She wanted no complications. He would survive without her as he always had done, and that would make it easier for her to walk away when the time came.

At the reminder of her departure, she dropped her remaining pizza in the box and jumped to her feet. "We'd better be going. I want to see my father before he falls asleep."

"Whoa!" Damien stood up and moved in close, frowning. "You still don't believe you're enough for me, do you?"

Her gaze darted away, then back. "Of course I do," she said, but even to her own ears she sounded less than convincing. Not that it mattered. Actually, it worked out better. If Damien thought she was upset over this, he wouldn't suspect she was upset over her upcoming departure.

A dark shadow crossed his features, but just as he opened his mouth to speak, some squealing children and a dog ran past them, kicking up the sand.

Thankful for the interruption, Gabrielle broke away from him and began collecting their things. After a moment he helped, too, but she was grateful he said nothing further on the way to her parents' house. For once, his running true to form like this...keeping his thoughts to himself...was working in her favor.

Yet just how she was going to achieve leaving him she wasn't sure. If she left without warning like last time, she'd have to leave all her belongings here. She wouldn't be able to pick up the threads of her old life. She'd been fooling herself to think that. Damien would be on her doorstep this time for sure. Pride would insist his wife come back to him.

But how could she start afresh somewhere and not tell her parents if she were to cut all ties? Could she really do that to them? If she only had herself to worry about, perhaps. But it was all so complicated. God, why had she ever agreed to come back here in the first place? She should have refused. It would have saved a great deal of heartache in the long run.

Fifteen minutes later she had to put her thoughts aside as she and Damien entered her old home. The front door had been left unlocked for them, and now they found her father lying in bed in the main bedroom, her mother reading one of the latest novels to him.

"What's this, Russell?" Damien said in a joking tone. "You getting soft in your old age?"

Russell chuckled. "It seems so."

Caroline closed the book and put it on the bedside table. "He tells me his days of reading the *Financial Review* are over."

Damien's glance sharpened. "So you're retiring?"

"Yes, son, I am. I want to enjoy the more important things in my life." His eyes encompassed Caroline and Gabrielle. "That's all that matters to me now."

Gabrielle's heart thudded. So many times she'd longed to hear such words, but now they only caused her more anguish and despair.

All at once her mother smiled a nice bright smile that went nowhere. "So, darling. When are you two going to have that proper ceremony? I'll need to put it in my calendar. I'm not sure where I'll be then but—"

Russell's eyes sharpened. "What on earth are you talking about?"

Caroline glanced at him, then away. "Um, I said I'm not sure where—"

"I heard what you said," he growled. "I'm just not sure *why* you said it. You're not going anywhere. At least not without me."

She flushed but held herself stiffly. "Russell, I came back because you had a stroke. Now that you're getting better you don't need me anymore."

"Wrong. I need you more than ever, Caroline," he said brusquely.

A tremor touched her mother's lips. "Russell, I—"

"Do you love me?"

Caroline's chin lifted as she met his gaze head on. "Why do you ask?"

"Because I love you," he said, the rough edge of emotion in her father's voice. "More than ever."

Her mother looked hesitant. "You do?"

"Of course I do." His gaze swept over them all, an arrogant tilt to his head that reminded her of Damien. "And I don't care who knows it."

Caroline bit her lip. "But…I didn't think you cared anymore. You've been acting so…polite at times."

"Only because I wanted to recover fully before convincing you to stay with me. As it is—" he looked down at himself on the bed, then up again "—I'm still not well enough, but I want you to stay with me anyway."

Caroline's eyes lit with hope. "You do?"

"Yes," he said on a broken whisper, holding out his hand toward her.

"Oh, Russell." She went into his arms.

Gabrielle's despair lessened at their avowal of love. Her parents would be okay without her. They loved each other after all. Love would get them through it.

As it would her.

Something pulled her tear-filled gaze away from her parents to the window. Damien stood, looking at her, his gaze penetrating and oddly watchful.

"Well, well, Russell," a male voice interrupted from the doorway behind them. "This is quite a development."

Gabrielle spun around and found Keiran standing there with a smile that oozed false charm. The torment of his presence sent sudden desolation sweeping over her.

"Keiran," Russell said, sounding pleased. "Come in.

Come in. I've got some news. I intend to renew my vows to Caroline just as soon as it can be arranged."

Keiran stepped forward into the room. "That's fantastic news. I always knew you two belonged together." He stopped beside Gabrielle and smiled across the room at Damien. "Just like I knew these two belonged together."

"Oh, so you saw it, too," Russell said, leaning back on the pillow with the air of a man who had everything now.

"I sure did. And it makes my heart glad for them both." He smiled at her, but his eyes were cold. "I'm sure nothing can come between them now. Don't you agree, Gabrielle?"

Her nerves tensed. "I—"

"You got that right," Damien cut across her from his position at the window.

Keiran inclined his head, but the smug smile stayed on his lips. He was in control of her and Damien's future, and he knew it.

Then Keiran looked down at Gabrielle beside him, making her jump when he lifted her wrist and turned it over. "Oh my, coz. How on earth did you get this nasty bruise?"

She'd been too upset to notice the bruise herself until now. It wasn't large but it was dark purple where Keiran had dug his thumb into her. Thankfully, it was on the underside of her wrist and hard to see.

Gabrielle snatched her hand back. "Um…I'm not sure," she said, darting a look at Damien and seeing his eyes sharpen.

"You'll have to be more careful in the future," Keiran said with fake concern.

Her mother moved closer and picked up Gabrielle's hand to check the inside of her wrist. "Keiran's right. That's a nasty bruise, darling."

Gabrielle could feel heat creeping into her cheeks. Her mother would be shocked to know that her nephew had put the bruise there. They would *all* be shocked. She found it hard to believe herself.

Keiran gave a light chuckle. "She tripped the other day and would have fallen if I hadn't saved her," he lied. "She always was a bit of a klutz."

Caroline frowned. "I don't remember that, Keiran."

"Me, neither," Russell said with a scowl, and Gabrielle's heart jumped in her throat. Her father was looking at Keiran with slightly narrowed eyes. Did he suspect the truth? Oh God, she hoped not. It would lead to dangerous secrets being exposed.

Her mother's face cleared. "How about I make us some iced tea?"

Gabrielle quickly forced a smile. "That would be lovely, Mum," she said, all at once knowing that Keiran *had* tripped her up the other day. It hadn't been an accident.

Keiran smiled at her mother, but Gabrielle thought he looked a little nervous now, as well he should. "Yes, that would be perfect, Caroline."

Gabrielle swallowed hard as her mother left the room with a spring in her step. Her father was still frowning slightly, but it was Damien whom Gabrielle was worried about now. His eyes were on Keiran with a lethal calmness that seriously worried her. She had the feeling he had caught onto what Keiran was doing.

* * *

Damien didn't know how he managed to get through the next half hour. He hoped to God he was wrong, but his gut was telling him differently. Tension coiled inside him.

"Okay, Gabrielle," he said once they were home. She'd been sending him wary glances on the way, and he'd done nothing to put her mind at ease. He wanted her to spill all, and he wanted no procrastination. "Tell me. How did you get that bruise?"

Seconds crawled by. She shot him an anxious glance. "Um…bruise?" she said, not fooling him for an instant.

He jerked his head at her hand. "The one on your wrist there. Or should I say the one *under* your wrist?"

"Oh, *that* one." She shrugged as she placed her handbag on the sofa. "I can't remember."

"Keiran knew it was there," he pointed out.

One delicate eyebrow rose. "What are you implying, Damien?"

They both knew she was hiding something. "Keiran was being a smart-arse about it. He doesn't do that for no good reason."

"That's just Keiran being Keiran."

He held back his irritation at her delaying tactics. "The thing is *why* did he feel he had to point it out?"

"How do I know?" she challenged, but there was something in her blue eyes telling him she wasn't nearly as defiant underneath. There was a hint of fear in her eyes.

His gut knotted more. "I think you do," he said silkily.

She squared her shoulders. "Are you calling me a liar?"

"Yes." He stared hard, letting her know he wasn't

about to give up. He would find out what all this was about if it was the last thing he did.

Suddenly her shoulders slumped just a little. "Damien, please let things be."

He expelled a harsh breath. "Jesus, did Keiran really put that bruise on you?" Even though he'd suspected, it was a different thing knowing for sure.

She wrapped her arms around herself in a defensive gesture. "Yes, Damien. He did."

A knifing pain sliced through his chest. "I'll kill him," he rasped, taking a step toward the door.

"No!" She stepped in front of him. "What's the use now, Damien? Let it be."

He stopped, looked down at her face. "Why didn't you tell me?"

"Because it didn't seem much at the time."

He swore. No one should put up with physical abuse, and certainly not from a weak-willed coward like—

"I wouldn't listen to him this morning, you see," she said, cutting across his thoughts. "He grabbed my wrist too tight, that's all."

He gave her a glance of disbelief. "All? He was gloating. He did it deliberately." Something occurred to him. "Hell, he was gloating over you tripping up, too. Did he trip you, Gabrielle? The truth please."

She winced. "I...I think so."

Damien's jaw clenched. There was more to this than she was saying. "Why wouldn't you listen to him? What was he saying?"

"Nothing. It was just about work," she said, but her eyes darted away again, making him increasingly uneasy.

"You should have told me. If he did it once he would do it again."

"I kept thinking he wouldn't."

"Not bloody likely," he rasped.

She sighed. "I know."

All at once he realized something else. Gabrielle had no trouble standing up to Keiran before. So why *wasn't* she standing up to her cousin over this? What did Keiran have over her? There was only one way to find out.

"Right." He sidestepped her and strode to the door. It was getting late but he couldn't stay here a moment longer without wanting to carry her off to bed and dull the thought of Keiran from her mind. And from his own. But tonight it wouldn't be enough.

"Damien, please," she implored behind him. "This is madness."

He continued walking. He was a man on a mission now.

"Damien, where are you going?"

He continued walking. "Guess."

"Damien, don't. Please let things be."

He stopped briefly and looked back at her. "No chance in hell." Then he walked out the door. He had things to sort out. And Keiran Kane was one of them.

Ten

Gabrielle watched Damien leave, sick with anguish. How could she have told him about Keiran's blackmail? He would have had to ask why.

And now he was on his way to find her cousin. What would he do when he got there? Would he actually hit Keiran? He'd certainly looked angry enough. Or would he be cool and calm and even more dangerous? Knowing Damien, it would be the latter.

Of course, Keiran wouldn't hesitate to tell him about the miscarriage. He'd even tell him it was another man's baby, though she could soon straighten that out.

What she couldn't explain was *not* telling Damien about his child. How could she look him in the eye and tell him she'd lost the marvelous little creation he hadn't known they'd made together?

She closed her eyes, her heart aching with pain. Damien was about to be blindsided, and she was about to lose the man she loved sooner than she'd expected. Dear God, she hadn't wanted to stir up anymore heartache, but heartache was definitely on the agenda.

Somehow she dragged herself into the shower before changing into her nightgown and slipping into bed. And her anguish turned to a different kind of pain when midnight came and went and there was still no sign of Damien returning. She could have called him on his cell phone, but a sickening thought brought tears to her eyes.

Had he gone to find comfort in the arms of another woman? Cynthia perhaps? He'd never explained who exactly that "woman friend" was and what she wanted.

Her father certainly had turned to other women years ago. It's what men did, wasn't it? When things got tough they went elsewhere. Would Damien come home smelling of Cynthia's perfume and with her lipstick on his collar? The thought ripped at her insides as she hugged Damien's pillow to her.

When first light came her heart was heavy. Damien must know about the miscarriage by now. He hadn't come home and his continued silence reflected that he didn't want her to stay.

It was time to leave.

Oh God.

And how did she tell her parents she was leaving? She wasn't prepared. *They* weren't prepared. Perhaps she could say she had to go back to Sydney to help Eileen? Just temporarily, she'd say. That would give her father more time to recover from the stroke so that in a few weeks when she didn't return, it may not be so hard on them. Not when they had each other now.

Okay, so it was a coward's way out, but she really *was* thinking of her father's health. She would do it this way and hope for the best for all of them. She couldn't see Damien telling them about her miscarriage. He just wouldn't do that to them.

But Keiran would.

She swallowed hard. Damn her cousin for putting her in this position. Well, if he wanted her out, then he would have to make a deal with her. If she left quietly, he had to keep quiet about everything to do with her losing the baby.

But her brief taste of victory soon disappeared when she remembered that she had to get through today first. She had to face her parents. She wouldn't think about Damien right now. She couldn't. One step at a time.

It was fortuitous, then, that she'd told her mother last week that she would come over and get some of her old things sometime. No time like the present. She'd go right now. She needed to keep busy, and if everything was about to cave in on her, she wanted some mementoes from her room.

Lord, this was going to be so hard, she decided, getting her empty suitcase out of the wardrobe, intending to fill it with all the things she hadn't been able to take with her before.

Her mother's eyes widened when she opened the door and saw the lone suitcase in her daughter's hand. Caroline looked beyond Gabrielle to the Porsche parked in the drive behind her, then back at her daughter, her eyes confused.

Gabrielle pasted on a smile and wondered how she could keep on functioning. "I'm here."

Caroline blinked as she tightened the belt around her silk bathrobe. "Darling, here for what?"

Gabrielle stepped into the house. "I thought I might get some of those things from my room."

Her mother looked taken aback. "What? Now?"

Gabrielle hesitated. "Is it a bad time?"

"No, of course not. I just didn't expect you here this early."

"I'm sorry. I rise early." She knew she should probably leave and come back later, but she wasn't sure she would have the strength to do this again. "How's Dad?"

"Feeling much better."

"Terrific." That was one good thing in all this mess. "I'll just go up to my old room, then."

Her mother closed the front door. "Stop in and see your father first. He's awake," she said, but her eyes were confused.

"Okay." Gabrielle went to turn away, then spun back and gave her mother a hug. "Mum, I'm so happy that you and Dad are back together again."

"Thank you, darling," Caroline said, drawing back after returning the hug, a worried look in her eyes now. Gabrielle couldn't bear it, so she spun away and took the staircase two steps at a time.

Her father looked surprised to see her there and immediately asked, "Where's Damien?"

She swallowed hard. *That's what I'd like to know.*

She pretended to appear nonchalant. "He went to the office early."

Russell scowled. "Does this have something to do with your cousin?"

Gabrielle tried not to show her surprise, but she suspected she didn't fool her father. "I'm not sure," she lied, before changing the subject to his health, then made her escape to her old room and started going through some of her things.

And that's where she almost fell apart. To give up all this just when she'd found it again was unfair. To give up her parents was tear-jerking. To give up Damien filled her with despair and desolation.

In the end she only took a few keepsakes. The rest could be thrown out. They weren't of importance to anyone but her, she told herself as she went downstairs to the kitchen to get a cup of coffee to fortify herself.

Soon she would go and tell her parents the news that she'd had an urgent call for help from a friend who'd helped her many years ago. They'd understand surely.

Her mother walked in as she was pouring the hot liquid into a mug. "I'd love some of that," Caroline said, brushing a piece of lint off the light-blue pantsuit she'd changed into and wore with confidence.

Gabrielle forced a brittle smile. "Sure," she said, and handed the mug to her mother, then got another one for herself. She loved that her mother looked so good these days. If only…

Caroline leaned against the marble bench and took a sip of her coffee before speaking. "You like our new kitchen?"

"Yes." Gabrielle's gaze swept the room. She noted the changes but they didn't really sink in. It was people that mattered, not things. People you cared for. People who—

"Is everything okay, darling?"

Gabrielle's eyes darted to her mother's worried face. "Um…I'm not sure what you mean."

"Why are you here so early this morning? Why aren't you with Damien? There's something wrong. I can feel it."

Gabrielle wanted to tell her she was imagining things, but that would only delay the inevitable. She put her mug down on the counter and took a deep breath. "Mum, I have to tell you something. I—"

"Perhaps you'd like to tell me too," Damien said from the doorway.

Gabrielle spun toward the sound. Panic flittered inside her chest, even as her heart swelled with love for this man. If she didn't know better she'd say there was relief in the back of those green eyes.

Then she noted how weary he looked. And unshaven, and he was wearing the same clothes he'd had on yesterday.

He stepped inside the kitchen. "Caroline, can I speak to my wife alone please?"

Caroline looked at her daughter. "Darling?"

Gabrielle gave a small nod. "I'm fine, Mum."

"Okay, but just call if you need me." She gave Damien a slight smile as she left the room.

Gabrielle squared her shoulders and met his gaze as soon as they were alone. "How did you know where I was?"

"A good guess." His eyes considered her. "Why did you take your suitcase and come here, Gabrielle?" he asked silkily.

She frowned. He'd been there in the hospital room

when she and her mother had discussed this last week. "I wanted to get some things from my old room. To keep as mementoes." No need to say why.

"You're not leaving me, Gabrielle."

That took her aback, even as she partly registered his words. "So you know, then?"

He started to walk toward her. "If you think I'm letting you go a second time, then think again."

She began to frown. "But Damien—"

He stopped right in front of her and put his hands on her shoulders. "No, you listen to me. You're my wife and you'll stay my wife. Is that clear?"

She wasn't sure what was going on here. Keiran must have told him about the blackmail, so if he knew about the miscarriage why did he want her to stay?

She frowned. "I don't understand. A baby—"

He went very still. "Is that what all this is about? Do you want a baby?"

She tilted her head at him in confusion. "Damien, did you go and see Keiran last night?"

His expression instantly clouded in anger as he dropped his hands from her shoulders. "I tried but I couldn't find him. I think he's gone into hiding. And so he should. I'll bloody strangle him when I catch up with him."

Her knees wobbled with a flash of silly relief. Thank God he didn't know the full story. There was still a chance he never would…still a chance that… No, she was being silly. She still had to leave.

Then she remembered something else. How she'd waited for him last night. "Where have you been all night, Damien?"

He frowned. "What do you mean? I stayed at the office and did some work."

"Really?" If only she could believe that.

"Didn't you get my message? I left one on the answering machine to say where I was."

She blinked. "But I was there all night and didn't hear the..." She paused. "Um, what time did you call?"

"Around eleven."

She winced. "Oh."

He frowned. "What does that mean?"

"I took a shower about eleven."

"And you didn't think to check the phone for any messages after that?"

"No. I was too upset."

The look in his eyes softened briefly, but just as quickly hardened. "Okay, I get it. You thought I was out all night with another woman, didn't you?"

She lifted her chin. "I considered that, yes."

He put his hand under her chin, making her look into his eyes, not allowing her to look away. "Gabrielle, I've told you before. I don't *want* any other woman."

It was weird but right then she couldn't *not* believe him. It was as if something had opened up inside her heart and made her see him as he truly was. He'd been kindness itself to her parents. And he'd married her out of honor for her father. He wouldn't be the man she loved if he was the type to be married and have a mistress.

"I know," she said softly. She loved him, but now that love had deepened and strengthened.

His shoulders relaxed. "Good. And perhaps we need to discuss this baby business."

Fear lurched inside her chest, even as she noted an oddly watchful look in his eyes. "Not yet."

He gave a jerky nod of his head that was touching. "Look, I have to go home and change, then get back to my office. Negotiations are taking longer than expected. The guy has to head back to England later this afternoon and there's still some things to be settled."

She was tempted to go home with him but they would only end up making love. As much as she wanted to spend every last remaining moment with him, his job was important, too, and she didn't want to mess that up further by delaying him. He'd already given so much to her father's business.

She nodded. "I'll stay here for a while yet. I want to visit with my parents."

A gleam of disappointment crossed his face as his arm snaked around her waist and pulled her closer. "I *need* to make love to you. Soon."

She swallowed hard. "There'll be time for us later."

"Yes." He kissed her hard on the lips, then turned and left the room.

Gabrielle's heart thumped loudly at the odd flare of something she'd seen in those green eyes. There'd been satisfaction there, and relief, too. But there'd been something else. Something that had looked like *need*, not *want*. He'd even said it himself.

Need.

A few minutes later her mother came into the kitchen. "Everything okay, darling?" Caroline asked cautiously, obviously having heard none of the conversation between her daughter and Damien.

Gabrielle took a steadying breath and pasted on a smile. "Of course it is. We just had a little tiff."

"I thought that was the case." Caroline's face brightened. "I'm so pleased you made up. Damien's a wonderful man."

"Yes, he is."

"And I'm so glad his upbringing didn't affect him at all."

Gabrielle's heart jolted. "His upbringing?"

Her mother's eyebrow rose. "He hasn't told you about his childhood?"

"No. Please tell me," she murmured, almost afraid to ask.

"Oh, darling, it was nothing horrific or anything," she said quickly. "So put that out of your mind. But I know someone who knew his parents. They were devoted to each other, pretty much to the exclusion of their son. Apparently they barely knew he existed." She drew her lips in thoughtfully. "I'm sure they loved him, but it was as if they'd used up all their love and had nothing left for Damien. I think that's why he strived so hard to become a millionaire and why he's so aloof at times. He's in control that way."

"Oh my God." Ignoring a child and pretending he doesn't exist was a form of emotional abuse. Was that why he'd said sorry to his mother during his delirium? Was he apologizing for just *being*?

Caroline clicked her tongue. "I shouldn't be surprised he hasn't told you any of this. Not yet anyway. He loves you but it'll take time to break down the barriers."

Gabrielle dismissed the comment about him loving

her. She couldn't ever think that. As for his aloofness at times, if only he'd hinted... No, she could see he couldn't do that. Otherwise he'd be letting go some of that control he'd fought so hard to maintain.

She expelled a slow breath as she finally knew what made Damien tick. It turned her insides soft, made her vulnerable yet strong in a way she'd never imagined. She savored the feeling, drew on it. It gave her the strength to get through whatever the future held for her without Damien by her side.

And then out of the blue, her world shifted focus and she found she was looking beyond herself. Hearing about Damien's background made her realize she would be doing the worst possible thing if she left him. After all, his parents hadn't needed him and had ignored him all his life. And now *she* was about to do the same thing by leaving. *Again.* She'd walk out and never come back, as if she didn't need him, just like his parents hadn't needed him.

And all because of Keiran and his greed.

Suddenly she saw everything with abrupt clarity, and she knew she'd had enough of Keiran's demands. She couldn't let her cousin throw his weight around and destroy their lives any longer. Damien needed her. She couldn't walk out on him, at least not until after she told him the truth. Then if he wanted her to go, as painful as it would be for her, she would.

But on *her* terms, not her cousin's.

Dear God, Damien deserved to know about the death of his unborn son and the circumstances surrounding it. *She* would want to know if the positions had been reversed, no matter how much it hurt or made her angry. She now knew it wasn't fair of her to keep that from him, whether he decided to destroy her father or not.

And if Damien did his worst—and please God he wouldn't—she had to believe her father and mother would still be okay. They had each other, after all.

Damien had no one.

Fifteen minutes later Gabrielle quietly closed the door to her Porsche and walked up to the front door of a small house nestled amongst the palm trees and ferns. It was midmorning and, as suspected, she could see Keiran sitting inside the living room. He was lounging on the sofa, watching television, as if he didn't have a care in the world.

Her mouth tightened as she pressed the doorbell. How dare he try and wreck her life and those of the people she loved. He deserved no less than what he got in future, she decided, waiting for him to open the door. The look of shock on his face was going to be priceless.

It was.

But he soon recovered. "How did you know I was here?" he demanded curtly.

She stepped past him and into the house. "You use people, Keiran. So I figured you'd still use an old girl-friend." She stopped in the middle of the living room and arched a brow at him. "How *is* Teresa, by the way?"

His eyes narrowed. "Get on with it, Gabrielle."

"I've come to tell you one thing. You're fired."

For an instant he didn't move. Then he gave a short laugh. "You can't fire me. I hold forty percent of the shares."

"You're fired," she reiterated firmly. She didn't care how many shares he held in the company.

He crossed his arms. "I don't think so, coz. Or have you forgotten that I'll tell Damien all about you? And your parents."

Her chin angled. "Do your worst, Keiran," she challenged.

Surprise flickered in his eyes before they turned cool and calculating. "Perhaps I already have," he said, sending shock running through her. "You see, I knew I'd blown it last night when I pointed out the bruise in front of everybody." All at once he glared at her as if it were *her* fault, then shrugged. "But no matter. I won't be coming back to Kane's anyway. I'll be selling my shares, and Teresa and I are going over-seas to live on the money. It should last us a few years, don't you think?"

At that moment, an attractive woman came out of one of the rooms, then stopped dead, surprise flashing across her face. "Oh, hello, Gabrielle. I haven't seen you for ages."

Gabrielle nodded her head, but she wasn't in the mood to chitchat. Not that Teresa wasn't nice enough. Older than Keiran by about five years, she was always the one he came to when he needed help.

Teresa frowned as she glanced from one to the other. "Is something wrong?"

"Very," Gabrielle said.

"Don't listen to her," Keiran snapped. "She's only here to—"

"Fire him," Gabrielle said, feeling a little sorry for

Teresa, yet the other woman must know the type of man Keiran was.

Teresa gasped. "*Fire* him?"

"Ask Keiran about it."

"Shut up, Gabrielle," he growled.

"Ask him, but I doubt he'll tell you the truth."

"I said *shut up*," Keiran said through gritted teeth as he stormed toward her. And then he grabbed her arm and shook her.

Gabrielle shrugged him off. She was too angry now herself. "Ask him how he's been blackmailing me to leave my husband and my family and all that I hold dear."

"That's enough!" Keiran suddenly yelled, lifting his hand and slapping her across the face. The sound of it ripped through the air, and Gabrielle's head snapped sideways.

It took a moment or two for the stinging to set in. And the shock.

Teresa was the first to move. "Keiran!" she exclaimed, pushing him away from Gabrielle. "What are you doing?"

Gabrielle's hand went to her cheek as Keiran recovered his balance then just stood there, staring at her. He looked as taken aback as Teresa did, but Gabrielle didn't have time to feel even the littlest bit sorry for him. He'd really crossed the line this time.

She took her hand away from her face and drew herself up straighter. "Don't ever show your face at Kane's again, Keiran," she said, and on that note she sent Teresa an apologetic look and left them standing in the middle of the room. She walked out the door and quietly closed it behind her with cool, calm control.

And that's how she felt right now. Despite the slap, despite knowing what was ahead of her with Damien, she felt liberated from the clutches of her cousin. It gave her the tenacity to keep on going. If she and Damien were to have a chance at a life together, everything had to be out in the open. They couldn't move forward until they put the past behind them.

She decided to go home first and put a cool cloth on her face to stop the stinging and redness. By the time she'd finished, Keiran's imprint was nowhere near as bad as she'd expected, though she suspected she might end up with a bit of a bruise.

Then she drove to Damien's office, intending to wait until he'd finished his meeting. If Keiran had done his worst like he said he had, she just hoped Damien gave her the chance to explain.

But by the time she walked into the reception area of his office, anxiety had taken hold. She wouldn't be human if she didn't feel worried now.

His PA was nowhere to be seen, but a slight noise emitted from his office, so she walked over to the door that was standing open. Perhaps his PA was in his office tidying up.

She gasped when she saw Damien sitting at his desk with a bottle of scotch open and a half-empty glass. He'd had his head in his hands but he'd lifted it when she spoke.

He looked at her then, and her heart faltered at the pain in his eyes and the paleness of his cheeks. As if propelled, she slowly entered the room and stopped dead in the middle of it, the fine hairs on the back of her neck standing to attention.

"Why didn't you tell me?" he rasped, the words sounding as if they were ground out of him.

Her heart squeezed tight. "So Keiran *did* tell you."

"There was a report on my desk this morning when I came back from seeing you." He swallowed hard. "It said about this idiot who ran into you with his car. About the accident. About you…your unborn baby."

It was slowly sinking in that he finally knew. Her legs went from under her as she found her way onto one of the chairs. It felt like all the oxygen had been sucked from the room. "I'm so sorry, Damien."

His eyes pinned her to the spot. "You had another man's child," he said harshly.

She blinked, trying to clear her mind. She'd forgotten he would think that. "No!" She took a deep breath. "It was *your* baby, Damien."

His head reeled back. "Mine!"

"The baby was yours, Damien. And before you ask, the condom broke that one time, remember?"

He sat there, barely moving, but his face said an awful lot about the pain he was feeling. She felt it, too.

All at once he pushed himself back from his desk and stood, turning around to look out the huge windows behind him, but as if he couldn't bear the pain, he spun back to face her. "Why the bloody hell did you run five years ago if you knew you were carrying my child?"

Her throat tightened. "I just had to."

"I wasn't good enough to be the father of your child, was I?" he said in a low voice, like it was something he should have expected.

"No!" She was shocked he'd say such a thing. Not

Damien Trent. He was born secure. He'd never had an insecure moment in his life.

But then she remembered his childhood. And she knew differently. She took a deep breath and uttered the words that could destroy all their lives. "My father told me to leave."

His eyes sharpened. "*Told* you?"

"He was drunk one night and bitter over my mother. He told me to take my things and get out and never come back."

He scowled. "But he would have sobered up the next day. Surely you must have known he wouldn't mean it?"

"I was scared, Damien," she said, seeing the anger burst into his eyes before she'd even finished saying the words. "I was scared that eventually he'd lose control and hit me," she said, blinking back tears at the mere thought of it. "I couldn't risk that happening." Not like it just happened with Keiran.

He went quiet. A muscle ticked in his jaw. "And yet you couldn't come to me?"

A flash of guilt stabbed at her. "No. You would have made me stay."

"You don't have a high opinion of me, do you?"

"I do now. I'm sorry but back then I could only think you were like my father."

His green eyes remained steadily on her face. "I would never, ever physically frighten a woman, sober or drunk."

"I know, but I was young and I was hurting and I was confused by what I felt for you. And I had no idea what you felt for me." She bit her lip. "I guess I didn't really need much of an excuse to leave."

There was a lengthy pause as he seemed to assimilate that. Then, "Why didn't you tell me about the baby when you came back? You've had plenty of opportunity."

Cold fear returned full throttle, but she had to continue on the path of truth she'd chosen. "I was scared for my father's sake. I'm still scared that you'll blame him for everything. You see, if I hadn't left home I wouldn't have been in that car accident and I wouldn't have lost our child." She took a ragged breath. "But as far as I can see he doesn't remember a thing. And he's changed, Damien. We can both see that. So please, please don't say anything to him. And please don't tear down everything that he's built. He's my father. I love him. I don't want to see him hurt."

He stayed silent for a couple of interminable seconds, his face giving nothing away. "And that was our child he helped to kill."

Tears gushed into her eyes. Despite her plea, he was going to take revenge on her father after all. "Damien," she choked. "Anger won't bring our baby back. Please, you have to let it go. If you don't, it will destroy you in the end."

He held himself stiffly while some moments passed. "I admit I'd like to do Russell harm right now." Then something seemed to ease inside him. "But I won't."

She gave a sob. "Oh, thank you." The relief was intense and it washed over her like a wave. Her father and her mother could live their lives in peace now. *She* could live her life in peace now. She swallowed. Except there was the small question of what was to happen between her and Damien now.

"So, you'd rather I think badly of you than your

father?" Damien said, bringing her back to the present as he finally moved and sat again on the leather chair.

"Yes." But she wasn't going to be a martyr about it. When you loved someone you protected them from harm. That's all she'd been doing. "There's something else I have to tell you," she said, wanting it all out in the open.

He stiffened. "What?"

"Keiran tried to blackmail me. He said I had to leave and not come back." She went on to tell him about it, knowing she had to be completely honest. "And this morning I went to see him at his girlfriend's house. He slapped me, Damien," she said, putting her hand to her cheek.

Damien sucked in a sharp breath as he came around the desk toward her. "The bastard," he growled, tenderly cupping her chin so that he could see her cheek, his eyes so dark she thought they might never return to their true green color. "Did he hurt you? Are you okay?"

Her heart softened even more at his concern. "I'm okay. But it didn't get him anywhere in the end. I fired him."

"You did what!"

"I fired him. I couldn't let him get away with it."

A flash of admiration crossed his face. "I'm not sure Russell deserves you." He dropped his hand but watched her in silence for a moment. "Neither do I."

Suddenly she felt like she was losing him. "Damien—"

He twisted around and walked back to his desk. "You're free to go."

She blinked. "Go?"

"Leave," he said in a brusque tone, looking up at her. "I won't stop you from taking your things and going back to Sydney. I won't contest a divorce."

Her heart squeezed tight. "Damien, I—"

"Mr. Trent," a male voice cut across her as a young man walked into the office. "They're ready to resume the—" He stopped short when he saw Gabrielle.

Damien inclined his head. "Thank you, Liam. I'll be along shortly."

The young man nodded, his eyes darting back to Damien. "Um, Mr. Marsden said he doesn't have much time."

"Too bad," Damien snapped.

"Yes, sir," Liam said, flushing, then left the room in a hurry.

Gabrielle looked at Damien. Time was running out, in more ways than one. "Damien, I—"

"You don't have to worry about your father," he cut across her. "I'll continue to work at Kane's and help out until Russell gets back on his feet. James can take on more responsibility, too." He picked up some papers and got to his feet. "As for me personally...no doubt I'll survive."

She went to speak, to tell him she loved him. It was on the tip of her tongue, but suddenly she could hear voices out in the corridor and the moment was lost. You didn't tell a man you loved him when he had people waiting and a major deal to close.

Damien strode past her, leaving behind a whiff of sandalwood aftershave. "Goodbye, Gabrielle."

His words ripped through her but she let him go, his

back ramrod straight, his mind already blanking her out. She understood him now. She knew he was hurting, and that the only way to ease the pain was to stop feeling at all. He must have done that many a time when his parents ignored him.

Only, didn't he know by now that the pain didn't go away just because you blocked it out? It was there and would always be there. Unless you came to terms with it.

Well, she wasn't about to let him block *her* out. She wasn't going to do what his parents did and leave him to cope alone. She would make things right between them. How, she wasn't sure, except that she loved him and she would find a way to show him how much.

The first step was not to let him push her out of his life, she decided, taking the elevator down to the under-ground car park where she'd left her Porsche. Maybe by the time she got home she'd have figured out how to go about things.

Damien didn't know how he was stopping himself from going out and finding Keiran and giving the other man a taste of his own medicine. God, how could Keiran have hit a woman, and his own cousin, too? How could he have hit Gabrielle! It was the sign of a coward and a bully, and Keiran had well and truly burned his bridges with the Kane family now. The new Russell wouldn't stand for his daughter being abused...not that Russell ever would have, despite his drinking problem causing Gabrielle to leave five years ago.

And if Keiran knew what was good for him, he'd better

sell back those shares to Russell and get the hell out of town. *He'd* see that it would happen. Gabrielle wouldn't have to put up with—Oh God, Gabrielle wouldn't be around.

She was leaving.

And, dammit, he was sitting here at this interminable meeting when all he wanted to do was go back to the apartment to see if she had truly left. Of course, there'd been no reason why she *wouldn't* have left. He certainly hadn't given her a reason to stay. It wasn't as if he loved her or anything.

Like an onrushing wind, all at once he realized he *did* love her. No second-guessing. No thoughts of denial. Just sheer certainty that she filled his heart and made him complete. She's the one he'd been secretly waiting for deep within his heart.

Love surged inside his chest as he jumped to his feet. He couldn't wait a moment more. He had to talk to her before she left. This morning he'd almost had a heart attack when he'd come home and found her suitcase gone. He'd gone to her parents' house, praying she was there, determined to make her stay. This time he would *ask* her not to go.

Striding around the conference table, he apologized to John Madsen citing an urgent family situation, handed over to his second in command, then left the room.

But as he rode down the elevator to the car park below the building, his gut twisted with panic. Five years ago she'd left without telling anyone. Would she do that again? She could even catch a plane to somewhere else and not Sydney. He might never see her again. God, he hoped he hadn't left it too late.

His heart in his mouth, he stormed into the apartment ten minutes later. If she'd gone…

"Damien!" she exclaimed, coming out of the kitchen with a surprised look on her face.

He strode forward and drew her close. "Thank God," he uttered, holding her as tight as he could, terrified of her leaving, never wanting to let her go again.

She pulled back and looked at him, a question in her eyes, asking what this was all about. "You didn't have to come home yet."

"Yes, I did."

Delight flashed across her face then banked. "But I would have still been here tonight."

"Gabrielle, you can't leave. I—" He realized what she'd said. His brow rose, as did his hopes. "You would?"

Her eyes softened. "Yes, Damien, I would."

He held his breath. "For how long?"

"For as long as you want me," she said gently.

A lump welled in his throat. His hands tightened around her waist. "Darling, I'm never letting you out of my sight again. Never."

A soft gasp escaped her. "Damien, what are you saying?"

His chest filled with love. "The first time I set eyes on you, you stole my heart. The second time, you stole my soul."

"Are you saying…" She moistened her mouth, then started again. "Are you saying that you *love* me?"

"More than life itself," he said in a grated whisper.

Tears swamped her blue eyes. "I never thought… Oh God, I love you, too. I wanted to tell you, but there was too much between us."

A tear spilled down her cheek and he wiped it away with his finger. She looked vulnerable, and he wanted to make it better. There was only one way he knew how to do that. His mouth slowly descended to meet her lips.

He kissed her tenderly, fascinated by how soft her mouth felt. Soft and warm and all woman. Yet something was different. Something that made his throat convulse with sheer wonder. *Love* made the difference. It was right there, in the open. Neither of them could hide behind their fears any longer, not even if they had wanted to.

He broke off the kiss and stroked her hair. "Darling, I'm so sorry about our baby. You went through hell and I'll understand if you don't want more children."

She shook her head ever so slightly. "I *want* to have your children, Damien. And with you by my side I'll have the strength to look forward, not backward." Her eyes filled with regret. "Can you forgive me for not telling you about the miscarriage?"

He put his finger against her lips. "Shh. There's nothing to forgive. We'll both always be sad at what we lost, but if we have each other, the pain can be shared." He kissed her gently. "This is the way our lives are meant to be. We had to be apart so that we could find out we belonged together."

Her eyes shimmered with tears. "I think you're right."

"I *know* I am."

Her lips curved even as she blinked to clear her eyes

of moisture. "Oh, I forgot who I was talking to for a minute, there."

She was the sexiest woman he knew. And she deserved to be teased right back. "Don't worry. I won't let you forget ever again." He swooped her up in his arms.

"Where are we going?"

He stopped to look down at the woman who had taken his empty heart and filled it to overflowing with love. "To our bedroom. I need to show you how much I love you."

Her eyes sparkled so brightly they took his breath away. "What a good idea."

He smiled at her. "I'm full of good ideas."

She ran her fingers along his chin. "You know, this all sounds like a takeover, Mr. Trent."

He kissed her. "No, a merger, Mrs. Trent." Then with everything he ever wanted right there in his arms, he strode toward their bedroom.

Toward their future.

Epilogue

Six weeks later, Gabrielle and Damien renewed their wedding vows in a moving ceremony in the back garden of her parents' mansion. As she walked down the make-shift aisle, her father looked so proud, her mother smiling through her tears. Eileen Phillips had come up from Sydney, along with her daughters, Kayla and Lara.

Damien's "family" was represented by Brant and Kia, and Flynn and Danielle. Gabrielle had grown to love the other two women over the past few weeks, pleased they had welcomed her into their own private circle of friendship. But more than that she was thankful Brant and Flynn had been there for Damien all these years when he had needed someone to love him unconditionally.

As for the man himself…she looked ahead…and there he was in front of her.

Damien.

He was so handsome. So *right* for her. He made her feel beautiful and special and needed, and she knew he would make her feel like that for the rest of her life. Love did that to a person.

Her heart accelerated as her father let go of her arm and handed her over to her husband, not as a symbol of possession like she once would have thought, but of love. She went toward Damien willingly.

Later, at the reception, after they'd danced around the wooden floor under the marquee, he drew her away from the crowd to a secluded area amongst the ferns. The tropical moon shone down on them through the palm trees as Damien pulled her into his arms. "I need a kiss from my newish bride," he murmured.

She wound her arms around his neck and offered her lips up to him. "And I need *you*."

Damien groaned and kissed her deeply, his breath becoming one with hers.

As were their hearts.

Long moments later he lifted his head. "Are you ready for our honeymoon?" he asked, his hands slipping down to her waist.

She nodded. "A château in France sounds wonderful." Yet she knew she didn't care where she was as long as she was with Damien.

His eyes wandered over her face. "You are so beautiful, my love."

"And you're so handsome."

He grinned. "I think we'd better leave so we can do further admiring on our private jet."

"Oh, but—" She could no longer keep something a secret from him. "Darling, I have something to tell you. I wasn't sure if I should. I mean, I don't know if it's too soon—"

His eyes flared. "Tell me."

"I think I'm pregnant," she said, hearing the excitement in her own voice.

He shuddered, then tenderly cupped her face with his hands. "Thank you, my darling. That's the perfect gift for a man who has everything."

Her heart was full as his head lowered for another kiss. She knew exactly what he meant.

* * * * *

Welcome to cowboy country...

Turn the page for a sneak preview of
TEXAS BABY
by
Kathleen O'Brien
An exciting new title from Harlequin Superromance
for everyone
who loves stories about the West.

Harlequin Superromance—
Where life and love weave together in emotional and
unforgettable ways.

CHAPTER ONE

CHASE TRANSFERRED his gaze to the road and identified a foreign spot on the horizon. A car. Almost half a mile away, where the straight, tree-lined drive met the public road. He could tell it was coming too fast, but judging the speed of a vehicle moving straight toward you was tricky.

It wasn't until it was about two hundred yards away that he realized the driver must be drunk...or crazy. Or both.

The guy was going maybe sixty. On a private drive, out here in ranch country, where kids or horses or tractors or stupid chickens might come darting out any minute—that was criminal. Chase straightened from his comfortable slouch and waved his hands.

"Slow down, you fool," he called out. He took the porch steps quickly and began walking fast down the driveway.

The car veered oddly, from one lane to another, then

up onto the slight rise of the thick green spring grass. It just barely missed the fence.

"Slow down, damn it!"

He couldn't see the driver, and he didn't recognize this automobile. It was small and old, and couldn't have cost much even when it was new. It was probably white, but now it needed either a wash or a new paint job or both.

"Damn it, what's wrong with you?"

At the last minute, he had to jump away, because the idiot behind the wheel clearly wasn't going to turn to avoid a collision. He couldn't believe it. The car kept coming, finally slowing a little, but it was too late.

Still going about thirty miles an hour, it slammed into the large, white-brick pillar that marked the front boundaries of the house. The pillar wasn't going to give an inch, so the car had to. The front end folded up like a paper fan.

It seemed to take forever for the car to settle, as if the trauma happened in slow motion, reverberating from the front to the back of the car in ripples of destruction. The front windshield suddenly seemed to ice over with lethal bits of glassy frost. Then the side windows exploded.

The front driver's door wrenched open, as if the car wanted to expel its contents. Metal buckled hideously. Small pieces, like hubcaps and mirrors, skipped and ricocheted insanely across the oyster-shell driveway.

Finally, everything was still. Into the silence, a plume of steam shot up like a geyser, smelling of rust and heat. Its snake-like hiss almost smothered the low, agonized moan of the driver.

Chase's anger had disappeared. He didn't feel anything but a dull sense of disbelief. Things like this didn't happen in real life. Not in his life. Maybe the sun had actually put him to sleep....

But he was already kneeling beside the car. The driver was a woman. The frosty glass-ice of the windshield was dotted with small flecks of blood. She must have hit it with her head, because just below her hairline a red liquid was seeping out. He touched it. He tried to wipe it away before it reached her eyebrow, though of course that made no sense at all. Her eyes were shut.

Was she conscious? Did he dare move her? Her dress was covered in glass, and the metal of the car was sticking out lethally in all the wrong places.

Then he remembered, with an intense relief, that every good medical man in the county was here, just behind the house, drinking his champagne. He found his phone and paged Trent.

The woman moaned again.

Alive, then. Thank God for that.

He saw Trent coming toward him, starting out at a lope, but quickly switching to a full run.

"Get Dr. Marchant," Chase called. "Don't bother with 9-1-1."

Trent didn't take long to assess the situation. A fraction of a second, and he began pulling out his cell phone and running toward the house.

The yelling seemed to have roused the woman. She opened her eyes. They were blue and clouded with pain and confusion.

"Chase," she said.

His breath stalled. His head pulled back. "What?"

Her only answer was another moan, and he wondered if he had imagined the word. He reached around her and put his arm behind her shoulders. She was tiny. Probably petite by nature, but surely way too thin. He could feel her shoulder blades pushing against her skin, as fragile as the wishbone in a turkey.

She seemed to have passed out, so he put his other arm under her knees and lifted her out. He tried to avoid the jagged metal, but her skirt caught on a piece and the tearing sound seemed to wake her again.

"No," she said. "Please."

"I'm just trying to help," he said. "It's going to be all right."

She seemed profoundly distressed. She wriggled in his arms, and she was so weak, like a broken bird. It made him feel too big and brutish. And intrusive. As if touching her this way, his bare hands against the warm skin behind her knees, were somehow a transgression.

He wished he could be more delicate. But he smelled gasoline, and he knew it wasn't safe to leave her here.

Finally he heard the sound of voices as guests began to run around the side of the house, alerted by Trent. Dr. Marchant was at the front, racing toward them as if he were forty instead of seventy. Susannah was right behind him, her green dress floating around her trim legs.

"Please," the woman in his arms murmured again. She looked at him, the expression in her blue eyes lost and bewildered. He wondered if she might be on drugs. Hitting her head on the windshield might account for this unfocused, glazed look, but it couldn't explain the crazy driving.

"Please, put me down. Susannah… The wedding…"

Chase's arms tightened instinctively, and he froze in his tracks. She whimpered, and he realized he might be hurting her. "Say that again?"

"The wedding. I have to stop it."

* * * * *

Be sure to look for TEXAS BABY,
available September 11, 2007,
as well as other fantastic Superromance titles
available in September.

REQUEST YOUR FREE BOOKS!

2 FREE NOVELS PLUS 2 FREE GIFTS!

Passionate, Powerful, Provocative!

YES! Please send me 2 FREE Silhouette Desire® novels and my 2 FREE gifts. After receiving them, if I don't wish to receive any more books, I can return the shipping statement marked "cancel." If I don't cancel, I will receive 6 brand-new novels every month and be billed just $3.80 per book in the U.S., or $4.47 per book in Canada, plus 25¢ shipping and handling per book and applicable taxes, if any*. That's a savings of almost 15% off the cover price! I understand that accepting the 2 free books and gifts places me under no obligation to buy anything. I can always return a shipment and cancel at any time. Even if I never buy another book from Silhouette, the two free books and gifts are mine to keep forever.

225 SDN EEXJ   326 SDN EEXU

Name	(PLEASE PRINT)
Address	Apt.
City	State/Prov.	Zip/Postal Code

Signature (if under 18, a parent or guardian must sign)

Mail to the **Silhouette Reader Service**™:
IN U.S.A.: P.O. Box 1867, Buffalo, NY 14240-1867
IN CANADA: P.O. Box 609, Fort Erie, Ontario L2A 5X3

Not valid to current Silhouette Desire subscribers.

Want to try two free books from another line?
Call 1-800-873-8635 or visit www.morefreebooks.com.

* Terms and prices subject to change without notice. NY residents add applicable sales tax. Canadian residents will be charged applicable provincial taxes and GST. This offer is limited to one order per household. All orders subject to approval. Credit or debit balances in a customer's account(s) may be offset by any other outstanding balance owed by or to the customer. Please allow 4 to 6 weeks for delivery.

Your Privacy: Silhouette is committed to protecting your privacy. Our Privacy Policy is available online at www.eHarlequin.com or upon request from the Reader Service. From time to time we make our lists of customers available to reputable firms who may have a product or service of interest to you. If you would prefer we not share your name and address, please check here. ☐

SDES07

Don't miss the first book in the
BILLIONAIRE HEIRS trilogy

THE KYRIAKOS VIRGIN BRIDE
#1822

BY TESSA RADLEY

Zac Kyriakos was in search of a woman pure both
in body and heart to marry, and he believed that Pandora
Armstrong was the answer to his prayers. When Pandora
discovered that Zac's true reason for marrying her was
because she was a virgin, she wanted an annulment. Little
did she know that Zac was beginning to fall in love with
her and would do anything not to let her go....

On sale September 2007 from Silhouette Desire.

BILLIONAIRE HEIRS:
They are worth a fortune...but can they be tamed?

Also look for
THE APOLLONIDIES MISTRESS SCANDAL
on sale October 2007
THE DESERT BRIDE OF AL SAYED
on sale November 2007

Available wherever books are sold.

COMING NEXT MONTH

#1819 MILLIONAIRE'S WEDDING REVENGE—
Anna DePalo
The Garrisons
This millionaire is determined to lure his ex-love back into his bed. Can she survive his game of seduction?

#1820 SEDUCED BY THE RICH MAN—Maureen Child
Reasons for Revenge
A business arrangement turns into a torrid affair when a mogul bribes a beautiful stranger into posing as his wife.

#1821 THE BILLIONAIRE'S BABY NEGOTIATION—
Day Leclaire
When the woman a billionaire sets out to seduce becomes pregnant, his plan to win control of her ranch isn't the only thing he'll be negotiating.

#1822 THE KYRIAKOS VIRGIN BRIDE—Tessa Radley
Billionaire Heirs
He must marry a virgin. She's the perfect choice. But his new bride's secret unleashes a scandal that rocks more than their marriage bed!

#1823 THE MILLIONAIRE'S MIRACLE—
Cathleen Galitz
She needed her ex-husband's help to fulfill her father's last wish. But will a night with the millionaire produce a miracle?

#1824 FORGOTTEN MARRIAGE—Paula Roe
He'd lost his memory of their time together. How could she welcome back her husband when he'd forgotten their tumultuous marriage?